BEFORE SHE COULD MANAGE A WORD, HIS MOUTH CAME DOWN TO COVER HERS . . .

There was no chance to do anything other than submit to that possessive embrace. His tongue probed gently at first, seeking purposefully before his lips hardened. Even if she'd had the inclination to resist, Patrick's expertise would have won her over. His hands moved surely, arousing feelings that she'd only suspected she possessed.

A moment, or was it eons later, he raised his head and brushed his lips insistently across the soft hollow below her ear. "Let's go over and try to get comfortable," he murmured, as he moved her toward the cot. "This is a hell of a place to make love. . . ."

D1570787

Other SIGNET Books by Glenna Finley

- [ ] THE MARRIAGE MERGER (#E8391—$1.75)*
- [ ] BRIDAL AFFAIR (#W8486—$1.50)
- [ ] THE CAPTURED HEART (#W8310—$1.50)
- [ ] HOLIDAY FOR LOVE (#W7823—$1.50)
- [ ] JOURNEY TO LOVE (#W8191—$1.50)
- [ ] KISS A STRANGER (#W8308—$1.50)
- [ ] LOVE IN DANGER (#Y7590—$1.25)
- [ ] LOVE'S HIDDEN FIRE (#W7989—$1.50)
- [ ] LOVE LIES NORTH (#E8740—$1.75)
- [ ] LOVE FOR A ROGUE (#E8741—$1.75)
- [ ] LOVE'S MAGIC SPELL (#W7849—$1.50)
- [ ] A PROMISING AFFAIR (#W7917—$1.50)
- [ ] THE RELUCTANT MAIDEN (#Y6781—$1.25)
- [ ] THE ROMANTIC SPIRIT (#E8780—$1.75)
- [ ] SURRENDER MY LOVE (#W7916—$1.50)
- [ ] TREASURE OF THE HEART (#Y7324—$1.25)
- [ ] WHEN LOVE SPEAKS (#Y7597—$1.25)

* Price slightly higher in Canada

Other SIGNET Books by Glenna Finley

Wildfire of Love

by
Glenna Finley

The wildfire dances on the fen,
The red star sheds its ray;
Uprouse ye then—it is our
opening day.
—Baillie

A SIGNET BOOK
NEW AMERICAN LIBRARY
TIMES MIRROR

SIGNET TRADEMARK REG. U.S. PAT. OFF. AND FOREIGN COUNTRIES
REGISTERED TRADEMARK—MARCA REGISTRADA
HECHO EN CHICAGO, U.S.A.

SIGNET, SIGNET CLASSICS, MENTOR, PLUME AND MERIDIAN BOOKS
are published by The New American Library, Inc.,
1301 Avenue of the Americas, New York, New York 10019

FIRST PRINTING, APRIL, 1979

1 2 3 4 5 6 7 8 9

PRINTED IN THE UNITED STATES OF AMERICA

For
Duncan and Eleanor

1

On such a beautiful spring afternoon, Carly Marshall normally would have been viewing the magnificent Alaskan scenery beyond the plane window without a single misgiving. Certainly not the niggling doubts which were diverting her attention even then from Mt. McKinley's icy splendor below on the left side of the jet.

She spared an absentminded look at the towering peak and then moved politely back so that a stranger sitting in the aisle seat could try for a picture. Even the appearance of North America's highest mountain couldn't shake the uneasy feeling that Alaska wasn't falling into the neat pigeonhole she'd allotted for it.

It wasn't as if she hadn't been warned. Her sister Nancy had been writing letters full of adjectives about the state ever since she'd taken a job there the year before. Carly, far away in her New York apartment, had ignored the superlatives and gone ahead with her plans for a Fijian holiday. Nancy could snuggle up to icebergs and polar bears all she wanted, but Fiji was the place Carly would investigate on her spring vacation. With any luck, she could even do some sketches which would come in handy for her job in the art department of a small publishing house. For some time, she'd been trying to specialize in illustrations for children, and the South Pacific backgrounds could prove valuable.

Her reservations for the island had been all set when Nancy had injured her wrist on a weekend cross-country skiing accident. It hadn't healed properly when Carly phoned later to check, but Nancy reported that the orthopedic man had great hopes.

"I'm coming to see for myself," Carly had said flatly with two years' seniority over Nancy's twenty-two.

"That's fabulous! But your Fijian trip . . ." Nancy obviously felt duty-bound to mention it. "You have it all planned."

"I know. Well, maybe I can change things around." Carly tried to sound as if it really didn't matter. "I could fly to Honolulu from Anchorage after I detour and spend a weekend with you."

"Fairbanks isn't Anchorage," Nancy pointed out. "It's another hour's flying time north."

"I'll survive," Carly said dryly. "One more hour is a drop in the bucket. Besides, the family wants me to make sure that you're really all right—otherwise Mom will never relax." Since their parents were currently living in Brussels on an overseas posting, Carly was the popular choice for an inspection tour. She went on, "Besides, Mom pointed out in her last letter that Alaska is practically on my way."

"Obviously Mother hasn't spent much time with an atlas," Nancy chortled, "but I'm not going to argue, since it gives me a chance to see you."

"Not for long. You sound practically back to normal and I still want to sketch brown babies and palm trees on my holiday."

"For one weekend, you can sketch sled dogs and gold dredges," Nancy informed her. "And there are other people here that I want you to meet."

Knowing Nancy, "people" translated to "men," and usually one in particular. "Don't tell me that you've fallen in love again," Carly said, having been subjected to several of Nancy's heartrending sagas in the past.

"I'm not going to tell you anything—until you get here. Let me know what flight you're on and I'll meet you at the airport. Have to run now—there's somebody at the door. See you, sweetie."

Carly was left with the receiver still at her ear, and she shook her head as she replaced the phone. Nancy might be having trouble with her wrist, but she'd bet next month's salary that a heart flutter was causing her more trouble. This was one time, Carly vowed, when her little sister was going to have to solve that problem on her own.

"Thanks a million," said a masculine voice close to her ear. "Would you like a print if it turns out okay? I could send it to you or deliver it in person if you're staying in Fairbanks."

Carly came back to the present in a hurry as the man with black hair and alert dark eyes who'd been photographing Mt. McKinley lingered by her place before returning across the aisle. "I appreciate the offer," she told him, "but my sister lives up here and keeps us well supplied with pictures."

"I see. Then I take it you're just visiting?"

His words revealed that he was going to try another approach, and Carly, who had heard a lot of them since high school and college, was polite but not encouraging. "A very short visit." Then, because he was a nice-looking man, she smiled and added, "It must be obvious that I'm a stranger. There wasn't anybody else in the Anchorage airport wearing a wool pantsuit when the temperature was in the eighties."

The man grinned sympathetically and lingered by the empty seat in her row. "On you, it looks good," he announced.

He could have gone on with his compliments, since she was the kind of brown-eyed blond that men dreamed about during long Alaskan winters. Her hair was the color of corn silk and flipped up at the ends just above her collar. An amber slide barrette held the soft strands back from her face, revealing high cheekbones and a straight nose above delectably curved lips. There was a chin which looked as if it could be stubborn on occasion—especially when the brown eyes remained cool and distant. The rust-and-black pantsuit she was wearing had tailored lines but it couldn't cloak the fact that her figure matched the perfection of her profile. He'd noticed that when he'd followed her aboard the plane after their Anchorage stop. Even if she was just staying in town overnight, he decided it would be worthwhile trying for a date. Especially since he'd also noticed that there were no rings on her left hand.

"I'd be glad to take you for a quick round of sightseeing if your sister doesn't have time," he offered. "I stay at a friend's apartment in town and I don't have to go on duty until tomorrow night."

"Thanks, but I—"

He cut in hastily. "If you're worried about formalities, I'm Craig Norbert. I'm a copilot on the Fairbanks–Seattle run for this airline." Her surprised expression made him go on to explain, "This is a deadhead trip for me because I spent my layover time in Honolulu. Fairbanks isn't in the same league for entertainment, but we could still have a good time."

Carly let her glance linger on his tanned and undeniably handsome features. There was a tinge of regret in her tone as she said, "Thanks—that's kind of you, but I imagine my sister will have made plans for me. It would be different if I planned to stay longer, but I'm headed for Honolulu and the South Pacific myself."

He grinned ruefully and started to say "I knew I came back too soon" when the pilot's voice came over the public-address system to announce that they were beginning their descent and expected to arrive at the Fairbanks international airport in eight minutes. The ground temperature was eighty-two degrees and the weather was clear and sunny.

"Which means that I'll not need this wool outfit here either," Carly said as Craig Norbert put away his camera. "Somebody should have warned me."

"People don't seem to think there's any warm weather in Alaska—just ice and igloos. You can find plenty of ice here in the winter, but we're fresh out of igloos. Anyhow, I hope you enjoy your stay in this part of the world, Miss . . ." He waited expectantly.

"Marshall." And then, when he still waited, she added, "Carly Marshall."

He nodded as if he approved. "Maybe I'll run into you in town later on—when you're with your sister. Fairbanks isn't a very big place."

She murmured something noncommittal and then forgot about it in the organized confusion that preceded their landing. Cabin attendants cleared away the last coffeecups and checked to make sure that all the seat belts were fastened as the muted roar of the plane's engines changed when they entered the final phases of the landing pattern. The cloudless sky made it easy to survey the broad Tanana Valley, bounded impressively to the south by the snow-covered peaks of the Alaska range. A wide dun-colored river which

Carly was later to discover was the Chena appeared to meander through the very heart of the city.

It wasn't until they had landed and she walked into the terminal that she remembered Nancy hadn't mentioned any specific meeting place. Despite what Craig Norbert had said about the size of Fairbanks, the airport building was crowded with people and the ticket counters were three deep. Carly thought of trying to page her sister and then decided to retrieve her luggage first. Nancy would probably come hurrying in at the last minute in her usual fashion.

As Carly waited for her suitcases to appear on the serpentine conveyor belt in the warm baggage room, she wished again that she could take off her jacket and stuff her topcoat in the nearest litter receptacle. The preponderance of travelers around her were masculine, and most of them were comfortably attired in cotton slacks or jeans and short-sleeved sports shirts. The few women in sight were bare-legged and wearing summer dresses or denim pants with tailored shirts. Carly decided that she was not only out of season but definitely overdressed, as well. She made a mental resolve to pay more attention to her sister's letters the next time and surreptitiously wiped her forehead with a handkerchief. Fortunately her luggage appeared before she had time to dwell on the temperature, but she'd no sooner retrieved her three bags from the conveyor than she was faced with a new problem.

If Nancy didn't appear soon, she'd have to phone or get a taxi and simply appear on the front doorstep. The latter choice sounded more appealing by then, but the taxi stand wasn't even within whistling distance.

She glanced around at the thinning ranks of passengers and discovered that airport porters were an extinct race in Fairbanks as well as luggage carts. Which meant that she'd have to leave one bag untended while she carried the other two out and tried to find a taxi.

After she lifted two of her cases, she hastily put one back down again. Change that to leaving two bags untended, she told herself in some annoyance, wishing to heaven that she hadn't been so quick in saying goodbye to Craig Norbert. He'd only been carrying one small duffel bag when she'd seen him disappear through the terminal door five minutes before. "With muscles to spare," she muttered.

"I beg your pardon," said the man who had come up beside her.

The combination of annoyance, frustration, and perspiration dripping down her back made Carly look at the tall dark-haired stranger with a hostile glance. "I wasn't talking to you," she said, and turned pointedly away.

She was tapped on the shoulder two seconds later by a none-too-gentle hand. "I hadn't finished," he said just as briefly when she whirled back to him, annoyance showing on every feature. "Are you Nancy Marshall's sister?"

Her eyes widened in disbelief. "How did you know?"

"I didn't." The fact that he'd found the person he was looking for afforded him no perceptible pleasure, because his gaze ran over her from head to foot and he appeared distinctly unimpressed at the conclusion. "I was told that you were arriving about this time."

"My flight was a little late," she began, and then tried to sound more friendly. "My sister can be hazy on arrival times."

"She wasn't on this one. I just had some other things to do first." He looked down at her feet. "This all your luggage?"

"Why, yes." A slight frown marred her forehead as she looked around him. "But where's Nancy?"

The stranger frowned back at her and then he ran an impatient hand through his thick hair, combed back sleekly from his tanned face. "According to Hal, she's currently halfway to Nome. Why the devil do you think I'm here?"

Carly rubbed her forehead, which was beginning to ache as a result of the heat and this latest *contretemps*. "That's what I'm trying to find out. Why the devil *are* you here, Mr. . . . er . . . ?" Her voice dropped in confusion when she realized that she didn't even know his name.

He wasn't chary about enlightening her on that. "I'm Patrick Donovan." The first flicker of amusement passed over his stern features when her confusion didn't lessen. "Nancy's landlord—but mainly an absentee one. I don't get into town very often." This seemed to remind him of something else, because he directed a frowning glance at his watch and added, "Look—there's some freight I have to check on. Stick around. I'll come back and pick you up when I'm finished."

Carly watched, openmouthed, as his lean figure in jeans and tartan shirt moved through an archway at the end of the baggage section. Then, because she was too tired and hot to do anything else, she sank down onto the top of her largest suitcase and stared smolderingly at the spot where Mr.—Donovan, was it?—had vanished.

If there'd been a plane leaving in the next fifteen minutes, she would have taken it. No matter how much was written about the ease of jet travel across a continent, there was a letdown at the final destination. Then, to find that Nancy had disappeared without bothering to even let her know—leaving a man who rated her lower than a freight shipment in charge of the welcoming committee—was enough to make a woman weep. Not that Carly had any intention of that, she decided, swallowing over the sudden lump in her throat.

Her determination was reinforced at seeing Donovan materialize in the baggage section again, lingering there as he held a laughing conversation with an attractive stewardess who was apparently reporting for work. It was only as he let his gaze wander around the room and encountered Carly's decidedly hostile one that he frowned and made another of his abrupt departures, leaving the stewardess looking after him in some frustration.

Donovan didn't bother with any explanations or apologies when he finally strode back to Carly. He swept up her bags and started toward the door of the terminal which led out to the parking lot.

Carly instinctively started to follow him. Then her Scots-Irish temper rebelled and she stopped abruptly.

Patrick got all the way to the door, automatically holding it open, before he noticed that he'd lost his passenger. His dark eyebrows drew together as he turned to see what had happened. Once his eyes lit upon her, still standing in the middle of the terminal, he didn't say anything. He didn't have to—not after a commanding jerk of his head and a glance that lowered the temperature in the baggage area by a good ten degrees.

Carly deliberately took her time in rejoining him. "Did you want me to come with you?" she asked in well-feigned innocence before he could speak. "You didn't say anything," she went on smoothly, "so I didn't know."

He shouldered the door open again. "I suggest we go outside and stop blocking traffic while we work things out. Is that all right with you, Miss . . . ah . . . er . . . ?" To her fury, he hesitated, obviously trying to recall her name.

"Marshall," she supplied with chilly emphasis. "Carlyle Marshall."

He nodded and walked to the curb, putting her bags down on the edge of it. "Well, Miss Marshall—so that we understand each other, I'm now going to get my truck." He spoke slowly and distinctly, as if she'd just touched American shores. "You wait here and I'll be back in about three minutes to pick you up. After that, I'll drive you—and your luggage—to your sister's place in town. Got that?"

Carly's look would have floored a less positive man. "I'll try to work it out, but in the meantime, what's happened to Nancy? Why isn't she here?"

"One thing at a time. I thought she called you last night to explain."

Carly's chin went up. "Well, she didn't. For heaven's sake, don't you think I'd remember?"

"I don't know." His tone showed that he hadn't been overly impressed with her intelligence thus far. "Just stay here, will you? I have to get into town—I'm behind schedule now."

He made another of his abrupt departures and left Carly staring after him. She found it hard to discover anything admirable in his personality, but she had to admit grudgingly that he was an impressive figure as he made his way around the arriving passengers. The tartan shirt fitted snugly over broad shoulders and then tapered to a waist and thighs that were lean and muscular. Whatever Patrick Donovan did for a living, besides owning the place where Nancy had her art gallery and apartment, it was a job that kept him in superb physical condition. Either that or he spent his spare time under a sunlamp, Carly decided, alarmed to discover the traitorous way her thoughts were going.

He was back, braking alongside the curb in a pickup truck before she had time to dwell on it. Without comment, her luggage was put in the back on a piece of plastic tarp to protect it from the dust of the truckbed. Then he opened the door on the passenger side and motioned her in.

Carly took a look at the high running board and uttered silent thanks that she was wearing a pantsuit rather than a narrow skirt. Even so, she wasn't a picture of grace as she struggled up and in. Donovan made an abortive move as if to boost her onto the seat when she was halfway, but she cut him off with a breathless, "Thanks, I can manage."

He looked sardonic but waited until she was on the cab seat before slamming the door and going around to settle behind the steering wheel. "I guess I should have brought the car," he said as he pulled out of the curving terminal drive and onto the highway leading to the downtown section. "In this climate we need four-wheel drive most of the year. The women who live here are used to scrambling up and down."

"I don't expect to be here long, so it won't be any problem," Carly replied, matching his offhand tone.

His jaw seemed to firm for a moment, but she decided she must have imagined it as he went on smoothly, "At least you picked the right time of year to come visiting. The weather's supposed to stay sunny and clear for the next week or so. That's one reason Nancy didn't want to miss this opportunity to get to Nome. She told Hal that it could be her only chance to contact some sculptor before the Eskimos move to King Island for the summer. Maybe you know more about that than I do."

Carly shook her head. Her thoughts were already confused at finding they were driving to Fairbanks along a smooth four-lane freeway. She hadn't been so naive as to imagine dirt tracks and dog sleds, but neither had she anticipated burgeoning shopping centers, attractive residential sections that looked exactly like their neighbors in the lower forty-eight, and residents dressed in California sports clothes. She rubbed her forehead again and tried to mask her confusion. "I haven't talked to Nancy since I left New York. She probably tried to reach me, but I changed my plane reservations at the last minute and made a stopover in Seattle. To see the jade collection in the museum there."

Patrick Donovan nodded without speaking.

Carly went on. "Who's this Hal you mentioned?"

Her question caused Donovan to shoot her an incredulous glance. "Don't you know?" Then, realizing that he was being redundant, he grimaced with annoyance. "I'm surprised about that. They were all set to get married last week but decided to wait until you arrived."

"Nancy's getting married!" Carly's voice was an incredulous squeak. "She didn't say anything—wait a minute—she did hint at something. Good Lord! She's never gotten this far in her romances before."

The truck swerved toward the edge of the road until Patrick quickly brought it under control. "You mean she makes a habit of getting engaged?"

"Well, not exactly. She's just sort of undecided."

"Unlike other members of the family."

She risked a sideways look, but he was staring straight ahead after that cryptic remark. Probably he didn't mean that the way it sounded, she decided. "How long is Nancy going to be gone?"

Donovan shrugged. "Depends, I guess. She'll probably contact you from Nome."

"Or maybe . . . Hal—is it?—will let me know. Will I see him today?"

"Not likely." Donovan sounded amused. "He's mapping claims, working out of our base camp in the Alaska range this week. That's about two hundred miles away—if there were any roads. I borrowed the copter to come into town this morning."

His calm pronouncements about far-flung places like Nome and the Alaska range made Carly realize more than anything else that distances in the state were hardly measured in commuter miles. Hopes for her Fijian vacation were disappearing even as she thought about them. If there was a wedding in the offing once Nancy reappeared, Carly would be lucky to get back to work in Manhattan on schedule.

"What's the matter? You look a little bewildered by it all." For the first time there was a tinge of concern in Patrick's deep voice.

Carly had no intention of confiding her misgivings. For one thing, she wasn't accustomed to men with such an assured, formidable manner. It was an effort to stay calm under that stony gray-eyed gaze of his, which had all the warmth of a granite slab when it encountered hers. The best thing she could do was simply accept his lift to Nancy's place, then say good-bye and make her plans once she sorted things out in private. "I didn't get much sleep last night because I had to catch an early bus to the airport," she said, trying to sound convincing. "When you add the six hours' time difference between here and the east coast, I'm not even sure whether I'm hungry or not."

"If you like, we'll take care of that," he said, letting up on the accelerator. "There's a coffee shop close by that isn't too bad."

"Oh, no . . ." She tried not to sound panicky. "I'm sure that Nancy will have left something in the refrigerator."

"I wouldn't count on it. From what Hal said, she had to leave in a hurry."

"Maybe I can go to the grocery," Carly said firmly. "There must be one close to her place." Then she remembered that he owned the building and undoubtedly knew the exact location of the nearest supermarket.

He wasn't long in confirming it. "There's a shopping center about a mile away."

"Well, then—"

"Except that there aren't any sidewalks," he continued, ignoring her interruption, "so it isn't an ideal situation for pedestrians."

"But I thought Nancy had a car," Carly said in confusion. "She didn't mention that there was any trouble getting around."

"I think she's been using Hal's while he's been out at the base camp. He left it at the junction when he hitched a ride on the helicopter back to camp yesterday. Don't worry—something can be worked out." He slowed at a busy intersection and turned left when there was a break in the traffic. "We're on the outskirts of the downtown area now. At least you won't have far to walk for any other kind of shopping. That's one reason Nancy wanted the place for her gallery. Apparently she's doing well with it."

"I guess so." Carly was trying not to think of this newest obstacle. It would be wonderful just to tell Patrick Donovan to drop her off at the nearest motel. She would have, too, if she hadn't remembered Nancy's graphic description of Alaskan prices, which took getting used to. Her sister had mentioned seeing an armored money truck outside the motel coffee shop on the day she arrived, and wondered what it was doing there. When she went in to breakfast and saw the prices on the menu, she was no longer in doubt.

"Are you sure that you don't want to stop for a cup of coffee somewhere?" Patrick Donovan was giving her another of his probing glances, and Carly realized the silence had lengthened between them again.

"No, thanks—I'm really fine." She made a determined effort to sound cheerful. "I didn't realize there'd be so much difference right downtown," she added, nodding toward a block where a log cabin was next to a modern apartment building.

"The housing's a real duke's mixture—just like the people." Donovan sounded offhand. "Of course, the suburbs are different. More like you'd find in the lower forty-eight. You're a little early in the season for the regular tourist activities, but maybe you can find something to occupy yourself while Nancy's away."

"I imagine she'd like me to keep the gallery open," Carly said, glad to find more familiar ground. "Probably she's left instructions."

Donovan was braking in front of a U-shaped two-story log house with a big stone chimney in the middle of it. The roof had the steep pitch Carly had seen on other buildings, and she remembered that temperatures sometimes hit sixty degrees below during Fairbanks' long winter. A neat sign by the front door advertised "The Gallery," and then Carly saw another door around to the side.

Patrick nodded toward it as he turned off the ignition. "That's the 'family' entrance," he told her, and fished in his shirt pocket for a key. "You go on in. I'll bring your stuff."

Carly realized there was no graceful way she could avoid accepting his help once again. She nodded and flinched visibly as he reached across her to open the door on her side.

"The handle's stiff," he said laconically. "I thought you might have trouble with it. Take it easy getting down. I'll come around if you—"

"I'll be fine," she said again, aware that she was beginning to sound like a broken record. She hung onto the door as she jumped to the ground, and managed to stumble only a little. Fortunately Patrick was going around the back of the truck at the time and he didn't notice.

She hurried up the path with the key in her hand, unable to miss seeing the "Gallery Closed" sign displayed prominently in a front window. The lock on the side door worked smoothly and she was partway into a cheerful kitchen when a spine-chilling growl halted her. She gasped as a huge husky appeared in an archway which apparently led into the living room. She stayed where she was, hoping that he'd do the same.

They were eyeing each other dubiously, with the dog still emitting a warning rumble, when Patrick came in, laden with her luggage.

In an instant the big husky's growl turned to a sharp bark of welcome and he bounded forward to greet the man.

Patrick recognized the difficulty instantly and said, "Take it easy, boy," even as he deposited Carly's suitcases in the middle of the linoleum. "Sorry," he continued, switching his attention to her as he rumpled the big dog's ruff. "I should have warned you about Toklat."

"It would have been better if you'd told him about me." She was surveying the big husky warily, aware that he still hadn't directed any friendly overtures in her direction. "Now I know what that expression 'dressed like a dog's dinner' means. I feel like the first course."

A slow grin transformed Donovan's features. "Don't worry—Toklat behaves a lot better than his namesake. In that case, you'd really have to worry."

"Toklat?" She frowned as she tried to remember. "What does it mean?"

"A light-colored grizzly bear that you find around the Toklat River up here."

Carly shuddered. "It fits. Are you sure this is a dog? The huskies I've seen hitched to dog sleds in the movies looked half his size."

Patrick wisely ignored her remark. Instead he took her hand and offered it slowly to the big dog. Toklat sniffed and then his bushy tail waved approvingly.

"It's okay, you've passed the test," Patrick said and promptly let go of her fingers when the dog settled back on his haunches.

"I'm glad. Do I dare ask what would have happened if I'd failed?"

Donovan's eyes narrowed as he surveyed her thoughtfully. "Maybe it's better not to." He stooped to pick up the suitcases again. "Nancy uses the down-stairs bedroom—right through here." He led the way to a central hall, announcing as he went, "The gallery's at the front of the house past that closed door. This is the sitting room—it was a den before Nancy changed the arrangement." He jerked his head toward another room opening off the hall. "Here's the bathroom—with a connecting door to the bedroom."

Carly nodded and went ahead to open the door when he paused at the next one, letting him precede her into a cheerful bedroom furnished with teak furniture. There was a royal-blue spread on the double bed, with the rug a lighter hue which blended nicely with blue-and-white drapes in a contemporary design. She watched Patrick put her bags down again and walked back to the hall doorway to ask, "What's up-stairs?" She gestured toward the short flight of steps at the end of the corridor.

"Another bedroom." There was a pause before Patrick shoved his hands in the back pockets of his jeans and added deliberately, "My bedroom."

"I beg your pardon?"

"I said, my bedroom."

"I know that," she replied impatiently, unaware that she was clinging to the hall doorway for support at this newest development. "You mean it was your bedroom when you lived here?"

"No—I mean it's my bedroom whenever I want to stay in town." His words came out distinctly, as if they were ice cubes tumbled from a tray. "Like tonight." There was another pause as he surveyed her, not missing how her expression went from stunned incredulity to definite annoyance. "Any objections?"

She didn't reply directly. Instead she said, "I'm surprised that Nancy agreed to an arrangement like that."

"She had to." There was an undercurrent of amusement in his voice then. "I wasn't anxious to rent the house, but this kind of commercial-residential space is at a premium in Fairbanks, so I could write the ground rules. However, you needn't worry about running into me very often, Carlyle." Then he added impatiently, "Don't people call you anything except Carlyle?"

"Not that I know of." She had no intention of telling him that her family hadn't used the name since putting it on her birth certificate. "Since we won't be running into each other very often"—Carly used his phrase deliberately—"it really doesn't matter. I take it that you don't work in town."

"Not at this time of year. We're out at the base camp most of the summer except when there's a special reason to come in. Today I had to pick up some machinery parts that we'd ordered from Seattle."

She hadn't expected anything else, but it wasn't encouraging to learn where she ranked in his priorities. "What about your dog?"

"Tok? He just came along for the ride."

"You mean he goes out to camp?" She surveyed the big dog, which was watching his master carefully from the hallway. "I thought he lived here—that he was another ground rule."

A reluctant smile creased her landlord's face. "No

such luck. He likes to follow the action. I just dropped him off here when I arrived in town. If he bothers you, I can shut him upstairs."

Carly matched his smile. "He doesn't bother me at all—if you can convince him that I'm not going to make off with the goodies."

"You don't have to worry. That reminds me, Nancy told Hal she was leaving you a note. It's probably in the den." He was leading the way back to the smaller room as he spoke, and hesitated for a minute in the doorway, letting his glance run quickly over the bookshelves which lined the room. Then he strode across to a small fireplace on the far side, where an envelope was propped against a brass candlestick on the mantel. "This looks like it." He turned and gave it to Carly. "I'll leave you to read it in peace. I have to get back to work." He started for the door, the husky at his heels.

Carly felt panic sweeping over her, and she hurried after them. "Just a minute, Mr. Donovan. What time will you be back?—tonight, I mean. And do you have a key—in case I'm out?" As he wiped his hand across the lower part of his face to hide his amusement, her voice rose. "It may seem funny to you, but I've never had a roommate before."

"Very commendable—all things considered." His voice was carefully polite. "At your age, too."

"I'm twenty-four," she replied, stung by his implication that she was tottering on the edge of senility.

His expression didn't change. "Amazing." Then, as she was still searching for a scathing reply, he said, "I'll be back about five. If you feel like it, we could have dinner a little later. There's a fairly new restaurant downtown you might enjoy. All right?"

"Why, yes—I guess so." His invitation, like all the rest of his movements, had been issued so quickly that she stammered in reply. Then, aware that her acceptance was hardly gracious, she said, "Thank you very much. I'd like to."

"Good. Come on, Tok."

Patrick was gone without a backward glance, closing the kitchen door decisively behind him.

Carly watched from behind the kitchen curtain as he opened the door on the driver's side of the pickup. The husky was up past him in an instant, to sit erect on the passenger's side, his tongue lolling in anticipation. Donovan didn't take much longer getting behind the wheel, and an instant later he drove off without a wasted motion.

Carly sank into a chair at the breakfast table by the window and ripped open Nancy's envelope.

"Dear Carly," the hastily written letter began. "You're probably ready to throttle me—leaving you to cool your heels like this. But the weather changed, so I couldn't miss this chance to see Quimealuk and ask to handle his work. His animal sculptures are gorgeous—so wish me luck! I should be back in Fairbanks in a few days. Until then, Hal says he'll take you on the tourist trail if he can get in from camp. If he can't, he'll find a substitute. (That's one thing about Alaska—there are scads of men to each woman! I can't think why they don't list *that* in the Chamber of Commerce publicity.) I'm sure you'll have a peach of a time—this place is full of surprises. Must run. Love, Nancy."

Her sister hadn't lost any of her enthusiasm, Carly thought ruefully as she folded up the letter. Only this time, Nancy was right on target. The place was full of surprises, all right.

One of them had just walked out the door, and at five o'clock he was going to walk back in. By then, she hoped that her pulse rate would be back to normal.

2

The sudden silence of the house seemed unnatural, Carly thought as she walked back into the bedroom and considered unpacking. She was reluctant to do too much, because if Nancy and Hal planned to use the place for their honeymoon, she certainly wouldn't linger on the premises. She wondered if Patrick Donovan would give up his landlord's quarters under those circumstances, and then shook her head in annoyance. It was no time to be considering idiotic questions like that. Not when a bath and change of clothes were at the top of her priority list, followed closely by lunch.

She managed the first two, changing out of her wool pantsuit into a pale yellow blouse and skirt that were cool and comfortable. The doorbell rang just as she found a pair of matching canvas espadrilles, and she slipped into them before going to answer it. She glanced through a kitchen window on the way and saw a man in his late twenties standing on the step. He was wearing jeans with a denim jacket and had a deep-billed cap shoved back on his straw-colored hair, which curled over his collar. Then she noted that he was holding a leash attached to a disconsolate Toklat at his side.

The dog settled all her qualms, and she went to open the door.

"You must be Carly Marshall." The man flashed an engaging grin that made her forget about his unorthodox appearance. "I was told to look for the prettiest blond in town."

"You mean Mr. Donovan said that?" she asked incredulously.

The grin wavered. "No. Not exactly. Nancy told Hal, and he passed the word along. Incidentally, I'm Wally Burton."

The remembrance of a paragraph from one of Nancy's early letters made everything fall into place for Carly. "Of course! You're the helicopter pilot! Nancy told about meeting you."

She stepped aside as he finally persuaded the reluctant Toklat to come in the kitchen, and closed the door after them. Then she surveyed the husky with some amusement as he flopped down in the middle of the linoleum. "I must say he went out the door a lot faster than he came in."

"He usually does." Wally unfastened the leash and then snatched off his cap as he suddenly remembered it. "Right now, he knows that he's being parked on the back burner and resents it." Seeing Carly's puzzled look, he went on to explain. "Pat and Laila were called into a business meeting at the bank, and she objected to arriving with a dog in tow. I told Pat I'd bring the livestock back here." Wally hesitated a minute. "Incidentally, Tok hasn't eaten. Would you mind if . . . ?"

Carly waved a hand toward the kitchen cupboards.

"Be my guest. I don't know where anything is, or I'd help."

"That's okay. Everybody in the outfit knows where Tok's food is stashed. Sooner or later, we all end up playing nursemaid."

She leaned against the sink counter, watching him reach in a lower cupboard by the refrigerator. He pulled out a bag of dry dog food and emptied some into a big plastic dish. Then he extracted another big bowl and filled it with water, putting it in a corner.

The sight of food inspired Toklat to get up and investigate. His aloof expression indicated he still wasn't happy, but would make the best of things. After one or two inquisitive sniffs, he lay down in front of the bowl, put a paw on either side of it, and methodically started crunching away at the kibbled biscuits.

"I hope Nancy left more than dog food in the house," Carly said, stepping around him as she opened the refrigerator door. She whistled softly. "Oh, boy— baked ham!"

Wally came and peered over her shoulder. "And cheese—followed by butter and mustard. In addition to being a red-hot helicopter pilot, I'm a very talented sandwich maker. Allow me."

"Thanks, I'd love to. Shall I make coffee?" she asked, after noticing an electric percolator at the end of the counter. "Or would you prefer something else?"

"Coffee will be great." Wally washed his hands over the disposal section of the sink before assembling any of the food. He turned to ask, "How do you like your ham—thick slices or thin?"

"Whatever's going. I never argue with the chef." Carly discovered the silverware drawer and started to set an oval table under the window after covering it with a cheerful turquoise linen cloth.

Toklat exhausted his dog food in short order and

moved over to watch Wally, who was collecting ham scraps on the cutting board. The husky waited, accepting two or three good-sized tidbits as his due, and then plodded over to the hall doorway. He lay down with a gusty sigh and watched them, his chin propped on his paws.

Carly was secretly amused at the way Wally tried to spruce up, carefully tucking his sport shirt in his tight-fitting jeans before coming to sit at the table.

At first she'd thought that he was simply an easygoing extrovert with little on his mind except fast answers and glib conversation. Then, as the moments passed, she realized that there was a sharp, considering look in his pale blue eyes which clashed with her hasty summation.

When she finished her sandwich, she rested her elbows on the table, holding her coffee mug idly between her palms. "Do you do a lot of flying for Mr. Donovan's firm?" she asked.

Wally retrieved a final potato-chip crumb from his plate. "Every day," he said, grinning, "and sometimes twice on Sundays. Depends how far behind schedule the fellows are. And the gorgeous Laila, of course. I can hardly call her one of the boys."

Carly's eyebrows went up. "You've lost me. Who's Laila and what kind of work does she do?"

"She's a geologist. I thought your sister had given you the rundown on most of the peasants who work with Hal."

"You don't know Nancy," Carly replied ruefully. "She's hard to pin down on solid facts. I gather that you, Hal, and Laila work for the same firm. What does Mr. Donovan have to do with it?"

"Lady, he *is* it. The 'yes sir, no sir, three bags full, sir' man in charge of the Arctic Resource Consulting Company. Also the main stockholder." Wally grinned across at her. "If you want to find gold or copper or zinc in this part of the world, come across with a handful of silver and buy yourself a field-exploration crew. Of course, we're a little expensive. The price tag on a helicopter alone is in six figures. Needless to say, Pat doesn't like his damaged—or his geologists. He's very narrow-minded about it, and so are they."

"I see," Carly said, beginning to understand where Patrick acquired his assured manner. "No wonder he acted as if there was a taxi meter clicking away all the time he was talking to me."

"That sounds like Pat." Wally's grin broadened and he leaned back in his chair. "He's not a man for relaxing during business hours. The only one who gets away with any monkey business is Tok"—he nodded toward the watching malamute—"and even he doesn't win all the time."

A slight smile flickered over Carly's features, but she kept her eyes determinedly on her coffee mug as she said, "And this Laila you mentioned—does she work in the office here in town?"

"Part of the time. When she can't get out of it," Wally replied. "She really likes to hover round the site where Patrick is working. The only one in camp who hasn't figured it out is our esteemed boss, and I doubt if it ever crosses his mind. Laila's just one of the drones during the busy season. Of course, he may work out a different arrangement in winter when everybody's back in the office. Laila's a might tasty dish, even if she does take herself too seriously." Wally's expression showed what he thought of that. "Now that you're up-to-date on the trivia, let's get down to cases. How about dinner tonight?"

His invitation was so abrupt that Carly almost let the coffee mug slip through her fingers.

Wally went on before she had a chance to answer. "There's a place on the edge of town that has a great exhibit of scrimshaw for the tourists, as well as serving good steaks . . ." He broke off as she shook her head regretfully. "You don't like steaks?"

"Of course I do. It's just that Mr. Donovan asked me to dinner before he left."

"Pat? Are you sure?"

"Unless I'm cracking up. Why? Doesn't he eat dinner like other men?"

"Yeah—but he was grousing about the million and one errands he had to do in town when we flew in this morning. I didn't think he'd find time for larking around."

"Larking around wasn't mentioned in the invitation," she said dryly. "As a matter of fact, I think probably he felt asking me out to dinner was the only polite thing for him to do. I gave him the impression that I'd blow a fuse on the electric can opener if he left me here on my own."

"And would you?"

"What do you think?"

"I think you might, if it suited your purpose." He rubbed the side of his nose thoughtfully. "I also think that Laila's found herself some competition."

Carly burst out laughing. "You've been looking at the northern lights too long or suffering from delusions caused by . . ." She broke off to ask, "What kind of delusions *do* helicopter pilots suffer from in this part of the world?"

"The usual ones. Blonds, brunettes, redheads."

"Those are illusions," she corrected and then blushed as his grin broadened. "I should have known. That's the second time I've been taken for a ride today."

"I couldn't resist." He stood up and carried his empty plate to the sink, rinsing it carefully. "Since you're busy at dinnertime, how about going for another ride this afternoon?"

"What kind?" she asked carefully.

He put his hand over his heart in a theatrical gesture. "A legitimate sightseeing trip wherever you want to go. Hal briefed us in camp that Nancy's sister is to have the best that Fairbanks has to offer while she's here. He'd be doing the honors himself if he hadn't been sent on a special mapping assignment."

There was no disguising the earnestness in Wally's tone, and Carly felt guilty of suspecting him. She should have known that Nancy's friends would rally round in her absence. "I'd like to go sightseeing very much," she added, getting up and carrying her empty plate to the counter.

Tok wandered casually over when the refrigerator door was opened again and would have poked his head in to inspect the contents, if Wally hadn't shooed him away.

"I'll be ready as soon as I get my purse," Carly said when the kitchen was put to rights. "Is what I'm wearing okay for our jaunt?"

"You look good to me," Wally approved, but then frowned as he considered her espadrilles. "I was going to show you over the rock tailings of a gold dredge. Can you manage in those?"

"If we don't go far."

"There won't be time for more than a general look-see," he decided after a glance at his watch. "Not if I get you back here in time for your dinner date. Don't worry—those shoes will be fine. Let's go, shall we?"

She looked at the husky, which had settled purposefully by the kitchen door as soon as the word "go" was mentioned. "What about Tok?"

"Well"—Wally rubbed the back of his neck awkwardly—"if you don't mind, we'd better take him along. The alternative would be to shut him upstairs, and he's apt to be a little stubborn."

"You mean, you'd have to take him by the scuff of

the neck and drag him up the steps?" she said, putting it more realistically.

"Uh-huh."

"That could take the rest of the afternoon. Besides, it's fine for him to come along."

"I hoped you'd say that. Pat's the only one who can really make him mind. Come on, boy." He opened the door, stepping back as the malamute whisked past him.

He was sitting complacently in the back of the pickup by the time they reached the truck. "Is it safe for him back there?" Carly asked as Wally opened the cab door for her.

"Sure thing. He's been doing it since a pup."

"He was riding up front when he left earlier today," she mentioned, wanting to make sure. The prospect of losing the dog was too horrible to contemplate. Rather than face that possibility, she'd hold him on her lap. Then she took a second look and had to smile.

"What's so funny?" Wally wanted to know as he waited for her to get in the truck.

"I was thinking of holding Tok on my lap—" she said, when he cut her off with a burst of laughter.

"You'd do better to sit on his. Don't worry, he won't jump out. Pat has him well-trained."

Carly was boosted into the seat, and he slammed the door behind her. When he came round to get behind the wheel she observed, "Mr. Donovan sounds as if he has everything under control. Does he get such instant obedience from all the people who work for him?"

Wally checked the side mirror on the truck and pulled from the curb before giving her a sideways glance. "You sound a little bitter, considering you only met the man today. What happened? Did he make you carry your own bags, or was he late picking you up?"

"Well, I didn't carry my bags," she replied. "You will admit that your boss seems a little sure of himself."

"He's as stubborn as they come," Wally announced, slowing to turn on a crowded arterial. "He's also one hell of a geologist and knows this country inside and out. That comes in handy with our weather pattern, so he doesn't have trouble getting people to work for him. This is my third season with Arctic Resources, and I can always find a job down south during the winter with a reference from Pat. Of course, I can see where he might be a little rusty when it comes to handling beautiful women."

Carly hid a smile by turning to check on Tok through the rear window. He was still sitting in the middle of the truck bed, apparently enjoying the scenery.

Wally continued with his favorite topic. "Other than Laila and a couple of the office staff, Pat's firm is strictly masculine."

"I don't think that would bother Mr. Donovan." Carly's tone was dry.

"I'm not so sure. He was mighty quick off the mark in inviting you to dinner. Maybe being out in the field has weakened his defenses."

"Don't count on it," Carly said repressively. Hoping for a change of subject, she indicated the busy freeway they were joining. "All my illusions about the 'lonely northland' are popping like soap bubbles. I hope we won't have trouble finding a parking space by the gold dredge."

"No way. As soon as we reach the edge of town, you'll see a terrific difference."

A few minutes later, Carly understood what he meant. Abruptly their road narrowed to two lanes and the houses became limited to small tracts. Most of the flat landscape was a combination of sparse underbrush and small trees, which Wally identified as black spruce.

"At least, there's no shortage of building property around here," Carly commented after they'd driven through a barren sector for some time.

"That's where you're wrong. This part is all permafrost—not worth a damn for building anything. Take a look at this road," he instructed when she appeared puzzled. "See where the potholes have been filled, and the uneven surface. That's what happens when the ground cover has been disturbed and the weather changes. It doesn't matter what's on top—whether it's a railroad or a house or an oil pipeline"—he nodded when enlightenment washed over her features—"there are always real problems."

"But they solved the permafrost problem with the pipeline, didn't they?"

"Sure. You can see for yourself, since we'll drive past it in a minute or two. Of course, it helps if you have several million dollars to meet the expenses."

She nodded and then exclaimed as the famed trans-Alaska pipeline came into view.

Wally obligingly pulled onto the shoulder of the road so she could take a longer look. "I didn't realize that it was so close to town," she said excitedly.

"It goes through all kinds of country in the eight hundred miles from Prudhoe Bay to Valdez. The beginning is what they call an arctic desert—afterward it crosses three mountain ranges, six hundred rivers and streams, and Lord knows what else."

"Somehow I thought it would be bigger," she said almost apologetically.

"Four feet in diameter." He looked amused. "It can deliver two million barrels of oil a day from fields that have as much as Louisiana, Oklahoma, Kansas, and half of Texas combined."

She made an apologetic grimace. "I should have

done my homework. Why is the pipe such a shiny silver color?"

"Insulation. And those supports keeping it above the permafrost are thermal devices to keep the soil frozen. That's to avoid those problems I was telling you about." He gunned the truck motor. "Had enough?"

"For the moment."

"I hope so. When I take a girl out, we don't usually end up discussing the chill factor or environmental conditions. Is there something special about you?"

She tried not to laugh. "I think I'd better change my lipstick or take up a new hobby. What about gold dredging—is that acceptable?"

"Now you sound more like a typical woman," he said as he turned back onto the highway and accelerated. "In Alaska, a man doesn't drag out his etchings after a date—"

"Let me guess," she interrupted. "He invites her to see his gold nuggets." She kept her voice solemn. "Aside from that dinner date tonight, I can certainly fit you into my social schedule."

He winked in understanding. "Ain't it the truth. There's nothing like discussing the price of gold to put everything in the proper perspective between the sexes. It's just lousy luck that Pat wants me to fly him back to camp tomorrow, so we'll have to postpone it."

Carly wasn't sure whether it was a matter for celebration or not. "How long will you be away?"

"You'll have to ask the man tonight. Probably a week or so, if all goes well. It won't make any difference to your plans, will it?"

She shook her head. "I'm just waiting for Nancy to come back."

"Then you should have plenty of time to come out here again and see things properly."

Carly wondered exactly what "things" he meant,

since they were driving through another deserted
countryside with the uniform pattern of stunted trees
on either side. There was a gentle hill in front of
them, and just before the highway started climbing,
Wally pointed out a monument to the man who first
discovered gold in the area in 1902. Several camping
vehicles were drawn up at the edge of the road alongside a creek, and the enthusiastic travelers were panning in icy water with more enthusiasm than skill.

"That looks like fun." Carly peered back at them as
Wally didn't slacken speed. "Where do you get the
pans to try?"

"Practically anyplace in town. It's not hard to find
color in these streams, but don't count on it for eating
money. You'd do better reading the want ads." He
peered at her. "Are you looking for a job?"

"Not at the moment, thanks." She was chary about
mentioning her artistic ambitions, since she was just
starting out in the book-illustration field and knew she
had a lot to learn.

"Too bad. We could use a stewardess on my run,"
Wally said.

"How many passengers does that helicopter of
yours carry?"

"Two or three generally, plus Tok, who likes to
travel in the first-class section," he added blithely, and
then pointed ahead of them. "There's the gold
dredge."

Carly stared with real interest at a boxy conveyance
almost two stories high, which was almost hidden by
the ridge of stone and gravel alongside. There was a
long appendage at either end of the dredge—a conveyor belt at the front, which transported the material
through the washing process, and a long metal
pipelike "tail" at the back, responsible for depositing
the waste rock after the process was completed.

Wally drove toward the dredge on a narrow rough

track which followed a rocky ridge. From the back of the truck Tok let out an excited bark as they lurched along. "He doesn't approve," Wally said. "I told you he liked his comforts."

Carly rubbed her elbow, which had just collided with the metal door handle, and sympathized with the dog. Fortunately Wally decided just then that they'd gone as far as possible and pulled up. He turned off the ignition and pocketed the key. "Come on, I'll help you up to the top of the 'tailing' so you can get a better view." When she gave him a puzzled look, he gestured around them at the rocky wastes. "Tailings are what a gold dredge leaves behind. These days, the environmentalists would have a fit." He got out on his side, whistled for the impatient husky to jump down from the back, and came around to help Carly. "Hang on to me," Wally said as they started up the steep slope. "These things are hard to walk on—or maybe you'd rather just stay here and sort through the rocks for a stray nugget. You might have better luck than panning. I'm serious," he said when she turned an incredulous face toward him.

She surveyed the acres of rock pile around them and shook her head sorrowfully. "I just lost my enthusiasm. Looking for a needle in a haystack would be a cinch in comparison."

As they reached the top of the ridge, she pulled her hand from Wally's to inspect one of the more colorful rocks by her feet.

"Quartz," he said dismissingly, turning his attention to Toklat, who had found a piece of wood and brought it over. "You're a pest," Wally told him, but heaved it obediently in the direction of the abandoned dredge.

The dog scrambled after it with a sharp bark of approval. Carly's glance followed him and then wandered over the metal sides of the abandoned dredge.

Down at the bottom, a battered door was half-open, although it bore a sign saying "Private Property—No Trespassers."

"I shouldn't think they'd have to worry about visitors," she commented. "It looks like an Alaskan version of a haunted house. I can hear the chains rattling even from here—and on a sunny day, too."

"Strictly your imagination," Wally reproved. He gestured toward the long rocky ridge they were standing on. "All the comforts of home."

She peered around them, not overlooking the muddy trickle of water under the dredge, and shuddered. "Charming. Let's go, shall we? Home, I mean."

"Might as well. Not much else we can do here—unless you'd like to look for nuggets or something."

"Another day," she said. "I forgot to bring along a burlap sack to carry them back."

He grinned and whistled for Toklat to follow them as they turned toward the truck. "In case you don't have time to come prospecting, you can visit the Gold Exchange in town. Normally they have some pretty good-looking nuggets for sale, although their stock might be a little low right now. Come on, Tok—get up there!" he told the dog as they arrived at the truck.

Carly waited until Tok was safely aboard and they'd followed suit before she said, "I didn't think nuggets were ever out of season."

Wally looked at her blankly, taking his attention from the outside mirror as he reversed the truck down the steep path. "What do you mean?"

"You said that their stock of nuggets was low—I thought you meant it was the wrong time of year to go shopping for them."

"Nope." He resumed his careful backing on the winding track. "I just meant that somebody did his shopping early. A thief broke into the Exchange last week and blew the safe. Walked off with about fifty thousand dollars' worth of nuggets. There's a reward out, I hear."

Carly whistled softly, leaning more comfortably against the door when they finally turned onto the highway. "I should think so. At the moment, my budget doesn't run to gold nuggets. I'd planned on something like an ivory letter opener as a souvenir. There's no shortage of them, is there?"

"Not that I've heard of. If you come out to camp, you can pick out a moose to send home. Or maybe a bear cub or two."

"Are you serious?" As he started to shake with laughter, she said severely, "*Not* about taking one home! I just wondered if you really got close enough to see wildlife at first hand."

"Sure. Sometimes too close. We had a couple of bears who had to be discouraged from joining us for breakfast last week."

"It sounds wonderful! Oh, not being that close," she assured him, "but getting a chance to see them in their native habitat. They'd make wonderful illustrations for a children's book. I'm sure I could sell the idea when I got back to New York."

"Selling it would be the easy part of the project. Unless you can cook."

"What does cooking have to do with it?"

"It's the only way I can think of to get you to camp. We could use somebody to fill in for a few days so our regular cook could get back to town. He's grousing about working seven days a week."

"I don't think I'd qualify." Her tone was rueful. "Aside from taking four gourmet cooking classes, I haven't any experience in that line."

"Gourmet cooking classes sound pretty good to me," Wally said, brightening visibly.

"But I didn't cook. I watched a chef do the work.

All the students did was take notes and eat the leftovers." Carly rubbed her arms to keep warm. "Maybe I can see some wildlife in town. The four-legged variety, I mean."

"There's always the stuffed brown bear on exhibit in the university museum if you're desperate. It's too bad that you can't come out and keep Laila company this week. Maybe Pat would relent, since there's going to be one female on the premises anyhow."

"You mean she'll be working at the camp?"

"I guess so. Damned if I see why she can't do her report here in town, but she must have caught Pat in a weak moment."

"At least she has an excuse for being there," Carly said, unconsciously waiting for confirmation.

"She seems to think so."

His skeptical reply didn't make Carly any happier. "I could ask Mr. Donovan," she ventured tentatively.

"Sure thing." Wally had to let up on the accelerator as the traffic thickened when they approached the outskirts of Fairbanks. He braked to let an oil-heat truck pull off onto the shoulder of the road. "After all, the most Pat can do is say no. Put on your prettiest dress when he takes you to dinner tonight. And if you have any spare time between now and then . . ."

She raised her eyebrows inquiringly.

"Bone up on a cookbook," he advised. "Who knows? It might just do the trick."

3

By the time five o'clock came around, Carly had done all she could to tip the odds in her favor. She'd fed Toklat again and left him snoozing happily on the hall rug while she'd changed into a burgundy ultrasuede shirtdress with a harmonizing foulard silk scarf at the neckline, hoping that it would be acceptable for the kind of eating place that Patrick chose.

When she heard the kitchen door open a few minutes later and went to meet him, it was obvious that he wasn't rushing to be ready for their date. He was reaching in the refrigerator to get a quart of milk and taking his time about it.

His eyes widened to see her obviously ready and waiting. There was something besides surprise in his expression, she thought, but it was gone almost immediately. Probably he was appalled to discover she was still on the premises.

Carly gave him time to think about it before she said, "You did mean tonight?" trying to keep her tone

pleasant and uncaring. There was no point in losing
her temper if she hoped to ask a favor from him later
in the evening.

Apparently she didn't succeed too well. His eyebrows went up then, and he walked over to pour a
glass of milk. "Of course. I thought we'd go about
six-thirty. It won't take me long to change. Can I fix
you a drink in the meantime?" He took a swallow of
milk.

His surface calm was disconcerting. Apparently he
thought that she was so eager for their date that she'd
gotten ready in the middle of the afternoon to be
waiting when he deigned to show up. A flush went up
over her cheeks, almost matching the color of her
dress. "No, thank you," she said, eyeing the glass in
his hand.

"This wasn't what I had in mind . . ." he started to
say and then broke off as he apparently thought better
of it. Instead, he swallowed the rest of the milk and
rinsed the glass before depositing it on the kitchen
counter. "Did Wally leave Tok upstairs?"

At that moment the big malamute walked in from
the hall, blinking sleepily. He wagged his tail at Donovan but settled on his haunches next to Carly.

Patrick's eyebrows came together at that. "Apparently he's found a friend. What did you do? Let
him empty the refrigerator?"

"He simply had dinner."

"I told Wally to feed him earlier. There was no
need for you to be bothered."

"Wally did feed him before we went out. Tok was
still hungry when we got back." Her hand went
down to fondle the husky's ears as he looked up on
hearing his name.

"He's always hungry." Patrick wasn't impressed. "If
I let Tok eat as often as he wanted, he'd be fifty
pounds overweight." Carly didn't reply, and Patrick

shifted his stance, realizing that he'd overstepped the bounds of courtesy. "I'm sorry. There's no way you could have known. I appreciate your taking care of him."

It was obviously the closest he was going to come in the way of an apology, and Carly felt relief at his gesture. "I was glad of the company," she said. "He's nice to have around."

A slanted smile warmed Patrick's austere expression. "I think so myself," he said, moving closer and gently shaking the dog's ruff. "Come on, boy. Upstairs—if you can make it after those extra calories." He softened the reprimand, telling Carly, "Give me twenty minutes. You might get the ice out. I'll be ready for a martini by then. Can I convince you to change your mind?"

"For a drink?"

His gray-eyed gaze met hers blandly. "What else?"

"Thank you. I probably will."

There was no faulting the manners on either side after that. The cocktail hour brought out a discussion of the weather and civic attractions that was noteworthy for its high caliber and boring content. Carly suspected that Patrick was as relieved as she was when he escorted her out to the curb after leaving Toklat zealously guarding the kitchen refrigerator.

"Although he isn't exactly a welcoming committee if you're a stranger," Patrick said as he opened the car door.

Carly nodded, remembering the ominous growl in the husky's throat before she was properly introduced. Then she noticed that Tok's changed attitude wasn't the only new thing. "What happened to your truck?" she asked, surveying the sleek black car in front of them.

"I left it with Wally. He had some things to pick up," Patrick added, dispelling any thoughts she might have that he'd changed transportation in honor of the dinner date. A minute later, when he'd slid behind the steering wheel and switched on the ignition, he said, "I should have asked if you like Mexican food."

She stared at him and then started to laugh. "You mean there's a Mexican restaurant this far north?"

"Sure. A good one. What's so funny about that?"

She leaned back against the seat, shaking with laughter. "Well, I knew better than to expect igloos at the airport, but I didn't dream I'd be eating enchiladas practically on the Arctic Circle."

"What did you think we'd do—concentrate on seals?" He sounded amused. "If you wanted a main dish of blubber, you should have gone on to the Aleutians."

"Thanks, but I'll settle for *frijoles refritos*." She kept her tone casual as he drove competently through the center of downtown Fairbanks. "What do you eat when you're out at camp?"

"The usual." Since the traffic was thinning, he managed a considering glance at her profile. "Didn't Nancy report on her last visit out there?"

"No. Not a word. I thought you didn't allow women visitors. At least, that's what Wally said."

"Since your sister is engaged to one of my top men and he wanted to show his fiancée around the camp on his day off, I certainly couldn't object. Besides, we were still in the slack season then." He was pulling up in front of an unpretentious restaurant on a downtown side street. "This is where we eat. It's not much to look at, but the cook comes from Juarez and specializes in some sauces that can take the top of your head off with one swallow."

"I'm glad you warned me," Carly said, nodding her thanks as he opened the door for her. She hesitated in a tiny dark foyer, peering uncertainly into a dining room where candle lanterns revealed that only a few tables were occupied. "It's like walking into a theater," she murmured. "Is this gloom for atmosphere?"

"More likely they're saving money on the light bill." Patrick nodded to an attractive young woman, who smiled and beckoned them to a table against the wall. "Hi, Maria! How's business?" he said as he pulled out Carly's chair.

The woman's shrug was more Latin than her costume. "It's early, Mr. Donovan. Ricky says we can't complain. There've been more tourists in town than usual." She was looking at Carly with frank curiosity as she spoke.

"This is another one. Carlyle Marshall, Nancy's sister," Patrick said, folding his tall frame into another chair across the table. "She qualifies as a special visitor, so I'm showing her all the best places. I've been bragging about your husband's cooking."

"He won't let you down." The woman smiled at Carly. "Is there something special you'd like?"

"I'll be happy with a cheese enchilada and refried beans," Carly said, knowing there was no use trying to read the menu in the gloom unless she asked for a flashlight.

Maria nodded, tucking the menus under her arm, and looked across the table. "The usual for you, Pat." It was a statement rather than a question.

"Yes, thanks." He turned to Carly then, as if he'd just remembered his manners. "Is beer all right with you, Miss Marshall? Or would you rather have something else to put out the fire?" He gestured toward the dip for the corn chips that Maria was putting in the middle of the table.

"Beer's fine," she said hurriedly, and waited until Maria had started toward the bar in the corner before she added, "It would sound more normal if you called me Carly."

"You said that your name was Carlyle." His reply

was offhand as he leaned forward to sample one of the chips.

She stared at the top of his head in some irritation, not wanting to admit that if she was going to wangle an invitation out to his camp on the strength of one dinner date, she'd better get their relationship on a first-name basis pretty fast.

"We discussed it earlier," Patrick continued, leaning back and chewing on the cracker reflectively. "I remember quite distinctly."

"I didn't know you then," she said uneasily, wishing the conversation would take a turn for the better.

"And you think you do now?"

"Of course not." She smiled, determined not to lose her temper. "But I hope to. From what Wally told me this afternoon, your job sounds fascinating." She saw one of Patrick's thick eyebrows climb skeptically and was glad to have Maria come back just then with their beer to provide a distraction.

By the time they were served and alone again, Carly was ready to embellish her story line. "The animal life up here fascinates me," she said as Patrick raised his glass. "It must be wonderful to work right in the thick of it."

"Oh, it is." He kept his voice expressionless. "Cheers!"

She looked startled and then hastily lifted her own beer glass in response. "Cheers!"

"Despite what Wally told you, we aren't knee-deep in Dall sheep, and we see a lot more rabbits than moose," he continued. "If you want to see wildlife, there's a pretty good selection around Mt. McKinley. I think there's some kind of a bus tour in the park. You can take the train down from Fairbanks."

Carly reached for a corn chip and stuck it in the dip, trying not to show her disappointment. Who wanted to take a bus tour when they could be smack in the middle of the wilderness at base camp? She decided to try a different tack as she absently bit into the cracker.

The hot sauce in the dip felt like a bonfire in her mouth, making her choke and reach blindly for her beer glass. "Oh, Lord!" she muttered weakly when she was able to quench the inferno and use her vocal cords again.

"Are you all right?" Patrick was half out of his chair in concern. "What can I get you?"

She sat back, shaking her head. "I should have insisted on seal blubber. My throat feels like I'd been auditioning for a fire-eater's job. You don't need one of those out at your camp, do you?"

"It's not on my list. I *did* warn you," he pointed out carefully.

"I know." She sounded rueful.

"Besides, I thought you had a job. Nancy told us about it when she was out at camp."

"She did?" For an instant Carly wondered whether she dared use her work to beg an invitation, and then decided against it.

"Of course. You weren't fired before you left New York, were you?"

She shook her head. "What made you think so?"

"You seem awfully interested in the job possibilities around here. Ah, here's Maria with our order. Just in time," he told the woman as she put their platters of food in front of them. "I was about to starve to death."

"Anybody would think you men never eat when you're in camp," the waitress chided him, looking over the table to make sure she hadn't forgotten anything. "Let me know when you want more beer. I hope you enjoy your dinner," she added to Carly.

"It looks wonderful!" Carly waited until the woman had gone across the room to serve another party before adding to Patrick, "I can see why you suggested this place."

"Ricardo wields a mean skillet." He picked up his fork and started on a generous serving of *frijoles*.

"Too bad you can't get him to take over weekend duty for your camp cook," she said between bites of enchilada, thinking how clever she was to have discovered an easy entrée to the next topic on her agenda. "I understand that he'd like to have some extra time off in town."

Patrick carefully laid his fork on the edge of his plate and took a deep breath. "You seem remarkably conversant with what's going on at camp. Since it's not like Wally to waste time on such commonplace topics when he spends an afternoon with an attractive woman, I can only think that maybe—"

She filled in the sentence when his voice dropped, "That maybe I was poking my nose into your affairs?"

The dark room made it hard to tell whether amusement softened his expression for a moment or not. All he said was, "I wouldn't put it that baldly."

"Stop being so damned tactful. I thought Alaskans were supposed to say what they meant."

He took a swallow of beer first. "All right, Carlyle Marshall. I don't know what in the hell you're driving at, but there's no room for visitors at our camp—especially female ones. It's enough of a nuisance when Laila is there on business. And if you were going to apply as a temporary cook—don't bother. Unless you could do short-order breakfasts on a butane stove at five o'clock in the morning."

"I wouldn't get beyond the first course."

"At least you're honest." He picked up his fork again and started on his dinner. "In case Wally used that old bromide about the geologists at camp being starved for female companionship, forget about it.

Their wives live here in town, and nobody's pining away. As a matter of fact, a couple of the men haven't used all the leave that they've accumulated."

"You don't have to explain," Carly told him, "I'm a quick study and I get the idea."

"I was sure you would."

After that, there was nothing discussed during dinner that was the least controversial. Carly asked about the gold dredges in early Fairbanks history and Patrick responded with enough information to carry them through the main course and into the delicious dessert custard that arrived afterward. He politely suggested a liqueur with the coffee but didn't comment when she shook her head.

He successfully maintained that impenetrable reserve until they were leaving the restaurant. They had just reached the sidewalk when he suddenly caught Carly's elbow in a firm grip and marched her into the dark entranceway of a curio shop instead of walking on to his car.

"Whatever's the matter?" she protested when he turned her toward the display window.

"Simmer down," he urged in an undertone. "There are a couple people I'd rather not meet just now. I don't think they saw us."

Carly relaxed and obediently stared into a display window full of souvenir items. She was still concentrating on some walrus buckles with "Made in Japan" labels when she heard a woman speak and then a man answer in a voice that sounded strangely familiar. A moment later a door closed and Patrick's grasp on her elbow relaxed.

"It's okay—they've gone," he said. "Sorry, I didn't mean to—"

"—get me out of the way?" She was enjoying his rare discomposure. "That's all right. Aren't you speaking to her?"

He gave Carly a sideways glance as they started down the sidewalk toward the car. "Laila? Of course I'm speaking to her. If you must know, she thought we had a date tonight and I begged off."

Carly's lips twitched. "At least she didn't stay home and read a good book. She must have found a stand-in at the last minute."

"Norbert." Patrick didn't sound enchanted. "I thought she'd gotten over him. I hope to God we don't have to go through another romantic saga the second time around. That's the trouble with career women—they can't separate their private lives from their professions."

"That's nonsense. You can't generalize," Carly told him briskly. "I know a male editor whose social calendar reads like a soap-opera script and we hold his head between affairs." She hesitated before saying thoughtfully, "Wait a minute—there was a Craig Norbert I met on the plane today. A pilot."

"That's the one." Patrick's tone was sardonic as he pulled up and started to unlock the car. "Craig doesn't waste time if there's an attractive woman around."

It was the second time he'd intimated that she was at least presentable, Carly thought with inner amusement. He must have approved of her appearance more than he let on.

She kept silent as they drove back toward the gallery, the deserted city peaceful in mid-evening.

Patrick turned left and drove along the street bordering the slow-moving Chena River, which Carly had noticed earlier from the air. There was little activity on its banks at that hour—little activity anywhere. Aside from cars parked in front of some taverns and eating places, it appeared that Fairbanks' residents found their nighttime amusement elsewhere.

Patrick's next comment showed that his thoughts weren't on the deserted downtown streets or the red traffic light which made him brake abruptly at an intersection. "What time did you leave Wally today?"

"I don't know—around four or four-thirty. He knew that I had a dinner date with you and wanted to change."

Patrick swore softly as a car came through the intersection after the light had changed. "Damn fool!" he muttered before starting up.

"I think it was safer at thirty thousand feet."

"Much. Getting back to Wally—did he mention where he was going when he left you?"

She thought about it and then shook her head. "Not that I can remember. He announced that you both were flying back to camp tomorrow. We discussed that for a while."

"So I gathered."

Her cheeks took on added color at his wry tone. "What's the matter? Has he disappeared into the wild blue yonder?"

"Of course not." Patrick wasn't enchanted by her flipness. "I *did* expect him to get in touch this afternoon. There were some things I wanted him to do. It just means that we'll take off later in the morning."

"Maybe he'll phone this evening."

"That won't help getting in touch with Laila." Patrick turned into a driveway behind Nancy's gallery. "I'll let you out here," he said. "There are cobwebs in the garage, and there's no sense in getting them on your dress."

When he came into the kitchen a few minutes later, she was filling the teakettle with water. He would have walked on through to the stairs without pausing if she hadn't said, almost apologetically, "I thought I'd have some tea—it's hard to go to bed when it's still light outside."

"You're not alone in feeling that way." He lingered for an instant in the archway and then came back to perch on a stool by the refrigerator. "Just be thankful it isn't winter and the other way around. When you only have four hours of daylight, you start feeling like a mole."

"Toklat must be making up for it now. He inspected me when I came in, and five seconds later he was back asleep in front of the couch." She was reaching in the cupboard for a mug. "Will you have tea or coffee?"

"Neither, thanks." Patrick yawned and got to his feet. "I think I'll follow Tok's example. I started at four this morning, and it's catching up with me."

His announcement sent a sliver of disappointment through Carly, but she didn't let it show. "Of course, I understand. Thank you for taking me out to dinner—I enjoyed it."

"Now who's being damned tactful?" he chided. "I thought you were the woman who believed in plain speaking. You might have enjoyed the food, but you looked like a spitting kitten when I said that there was no room for visitors in the field."

Her chin went up. "That was because you made me feel like a camp follower. I was simply interested in seeing the country, and Wally said that—"

He interrupted promptly. "Spare me what Wally said. I'll have words with him tomorrow."

Pride made her voice stiffer than usual. "I wish you wouldn't. He was trying to help, and I don't want to get him into trouble."

"Don't worry. Flogging hasn't been practiced around here for years. I have no intention of embarrassing Wally in front of Laila, and by the time we get back to camp, it will be old news."

Carly fastened on the only part of his announcement that really interested her. "You mean that . . . Laila, is it?—"

"Laila Anson. What about her?"

"You mean that she's going out to the camp with you tomorrow?"

"That's right. And she's coming back to town just as soon as she gets finished with a report. Although I'll be damned if it's any of your affair."

Carly walked over to the window and stared blindly through the curtain at the deserted street, determined not to let him know the sudden unreasoning anger that coursed through her. At that moment she would have liked to take the carved wooden bowl that Nancy was using as a centerpiece on the kitchen table and pitch it at Patrick Donovan's stubborn jaw.

Although Patrick couldn't know the violence of her thoughts, her sudden stillness made him realize that he had blundered. After all, she was Nancy's sister, he remembered belatedly, and as such, she was entitled to better treatment. He ran a hand over the back of his neck, wishing that she wasn't so damned beautiful and that he wasn't so damned tired. He took a step toward her and then stopped before he got in more trouble. "I'm sorry, Carly." His tone was deep. "I guess both of us have had a rough day."

His tentative peace offering prompted her to walk slowly over and face him. For the first time she noticed that the lines around his eyes were etched with fatigue and that there was a drawn look to his face. "I'm sorry to have hassled you," she said candidly. "Normally I don't go about wangling invitations when I'm not wanted."

He shook his head. "You've got it all wrong. I might not want you along, but that doesn't mean I don't want you. No—that's a hell of a way to put it. You're a beautiful woman and I desire you—which is something quite different."

Her palms went up to her hot cheeks. "Oh, please, I wish you wouldn't—"

Patrick cut her off as if she hadn't spoken. "Right

now, I haven't the time to do anything about it, so you can relax. Lock your door if you want, but it won't be necessary." He looked even more cynical than usual as he went on. "I'm sorry we had to meet just now, at—what's the expression all the bureaucrats use?—'at this point in time.'" He hesitated and then went on softly, "The next time I'm in New York, we might arrange a more satisfactory conclusion. Now, we'd better call it a night. You can have Toklat if you like."

"Thanks very much." There was a matching wealth of sarcasm in her tone. His calm assumption that she'd fall into his arms when he managed to spare time on a visit to New York roused her temper. He might as well learn that she wasn't a decorative plaything to be fitted into his schedule. "Exactly what am I supposed to do with your dog?"

"Keep him in front of your door," Patrick said, "in case you're worried about intruders." For the first time his voice sounded as if he were losing his composure. "Malamutes don't like to be disturbed when they're sleeping."

"I'll remember, but you'd better keep him by your door. That way you can be sure to get back to camp in mint condition. Otherwise, who knows? I might walk in my sleep."

His eyes glinted as if weighing the odds. "Do you?"

"So far, I've never been tempted. And never without an engraved invitation, so you don't have to worry." The last was added politely.

Patrick's jaw was so tight that it looked like a copy from Mt. Rushmore. His expression showed that if he'd ever felt any sympathy for her, it was long past. "I won't lose any sleep over it, I promise you." He walked to the hallway and called, "C'mon, Tok—time for you to go out. Hurry up—I'll take you round the block."

"There's nothing like physical exercise to solve all your problems," Carly said, going over to open the kitchen door for him. "Have you tried jogging?"

"I'll remember if I need a new hobby. It's a good thing you aren't coming to camp," he said, leaning over to snap a lead on Toklat's collar as the dog waited patiently. "You'd probably shove me out of the helicopter as soon as we got off the ground."

Carly turned her back disdainfully as he started out the door, showing what she thought of that remark. She had just taken a step toward the stove to rescue the teakettle when suddenly there was an angry whine of a bullet. At the same instant the glass windowpane over the table cracked loudly and shattered onto the linoleum. Her startled gasp coincided with a thud on the outside step and then a frenzied barking.

"Patrick!" Her lips hardly moved but her word was a moan of despair.

After that her movements were pure instinct. She dashed to the door and yanked it wide, to find Patrick crumpled on the porch step. He sprawled awkwardly back onto the kitchen floor even as he hung onto the leash, trying to subdue a plunging and whining Toklat. The big dog was doing his best to get loose, but Patrick managed to pull him inside and slammed the door behind them. Then he turned to Carly and issued a brusque "Get down, dammit. Stay away from that glass."

She didn't move. Instead she was staring at the red stain dripping down his hand onto the linoleum. "Blood! Oh, Lord—you're hurt. Come here, let me—"

He waved her back impatiently with his other hand. "Stay down, I said. He might still be out there."

"Who might be?" she whispered in bewilderment.

The sudden revving of an engine answered her, and then there was the shriek of tires as a car took off somewhere nearby.

The sound was evidently what Patrick was listening for. He waited an instant longer and then cautiously opened the door. When nothing happened, he nodded and closed it again—letting out a sigh as he did. "All clear, I guess. Thank God. We were sitting ducks."

"But what happened?"

"Probably just a drunk shooting up the place, pretending it was the Fourth of July."

Toklat went over to his water dish, still trailing his leash from his collar. Patrick roused himself to go and unsnap it. He stuffed it in his jacket pocket and said, "I'd better borrow a towel. Otherwise I'll drip blood all over the stairs."

"You sit down," Carly said fiercely. "Take off your jacket and let me see that arm."

"Don't get upset." Patrick was holding his hand over the sink by then. "This is just a scratch. I caught a glass splinter, not a bullet."

Carly was watching him carefully. "Are you sure they weren't deliberately aiming this way?"

"Well, Toklat has a limited acquaintance in town, and I haven't been around much for the past few weeks." Patrick gave Carly a thoughtful look. "I had the feeling that you were pretty mad when I went out the door. Are you sure you didn't put out a contract on me?"

Carly appraised the shattered glass on the linoleum before she pulled a clean linen towel from the rack on the door and handed it to him to wrap around his forearm. "I don't really think that's funny."

"You're right. I apologize." He shook his head wearily and started toward the stairs. "Better make that a blanket apology—there may be worse to come."

"What could be worse than getting shot?" she asked, wide-eyed.

"Well, the only thing that's left on the list tonight

is a monumental hangover. Right now, though, I don't think I have the strength to get drunk."

Carly didn't give Patrick a chance to carry through on his threat while she was around. After shutting Toklat in the upstairs bedroom, he allowed her to cleanse and bandage the unpleasant but superficial cut on his arm. When she suggested he see a doctor, he made a rude noise and said, "That won't be necessary. I've had lots worse."

She paused in the midst of clearing away the blood-ied cotton swabs. "Maybe so. But it could get infect-ed, and you're going to be out at camp."

"Wally could fly me back long before gangrene sets in."

"You needn't snarl."

"You're right. I'll see how it is in the morning," he temporized wearily. "In the meantime, I apologize—again."

She made an embarrassed movement. "I didn't mean to sound like a mother hen. It's just that I'm not used to being shot at—even if I do live in New York. Nancy didn't tell me that Fairbanks had urban prob-lems."

"Urban problems, hell!" he exploded, and then caught sight of her expression. "Sorry. Apparently I've lost my sense of humor."

"It's understandable." She washed her hands and dried them. "Are you going to call the police?"

"That's next on the list, but it's just practice, so there's no use hurrying. Whoever it was is miles away by now."

Carly nodded, remembering the sound of the car engine being raced.

"I'll call and report it, though," Patrick said. He looked undecided about what to do with the stained kitchen towel he was still holding.

Carly plucked it from his fingers and started toward

the utility room. "I'll take this and soak it. Are you going to keep Toklat incarcerated upstairs?"

"Might as well. After I call the police, I'll sweep up that glass on the linoleum. You stay away from it, too."

"All right. Let me know when the 'all clear' sounds. I could use that cup of tea I was making a million years ago."

It took time for Patrick to phone in the report to the police and sweep all the broken glass from the kitchen floor. Still longer for him to unearth a piece of plywood and cover the broken window frame with it. By then Carly was almost as weary as he looked, and she offered to call a glass company to fix the window when she got up in the morning.

"That would save me time," Patrick said finally as he lingered on the stairs. "I'll leave a duplicate set of car keys on the hall table. You might as well have the use of it while I'm gone. Somebody from the office will drive it back from the airport after I leave."

"That would be wonderful. You're sure you don't mind?"

"I will, if I come back and find all four fenders missing."

"I'll try to keep it under eighty except on the freeways. When do you think you'll be back in town?"

She was careful to make her question sound like a casual afterthought, but he gave her a sharp look over the stair banister. "I'm not sure. Why?" he asked.

"Nothing special. To be safe, I'd better thank you for the use of the car now, in case I've gone before your next trip."

He appeared startled at her words, but an instant later his impassive expression was back in place. "Nancy told Hal that you'd be here awhile. He said that she was counting on a maid of honor. Of course," Patrick added, staying stubbornly where he was on the stairs, "she might have to change her plans after this Nome jaunt. She can't expect you to sit around Fairbanks for your whole vacation."

"My feeling exactly." Carly was pleased to note that her hints about the dearth of sketching possibilities hadn't gone unnoticed. Ignored, she decided, but not unnoticed. "At any rate, thank you for dinner and the transport." She hesitated for a moment, wondering whether he was going to stay halfway up the stairs or come down and shake hands. She was pretty certain those were the only two courses of action left to him under the circumstances. There was nothing like being shot at for taking the bloom off a possible romantic leave-taking.

She would have been amused to know that Patrick was thinking the same thing. He was strangely reluctant to say good night, despite all they'd been through. Carly was extraordinarily lovely, and the light of the hall lamp made a shining nimbus of her blond hair. Her smooth skin was pale and fragile above the vibrant burgundy shade of her dress, and he had to move his gaze upward from the deep V neckline with an almost physical effort. What in the hell was the matter with him? he wondered. It was after midnight, he had to be up at four-thirty in the morning to get out to the airport, and his arm throbbed like the devil. On the other hand, a good-night kiss wouldn't hurt anything—but it would be hard to stop at one kiss when the woman was Carly Marshall.

He took a deep breath and let it out deliberately. "All the thanks should be on my side," he said. "I'll try not to wake you in the morning when I go out. Enjoy your Alaskan vacation, Carly."

Carly noted that he didn't look back as he went up the stairs. She had plenty of time to make sure, because her feet dragged as she walked to her own bedroom door. The sound of Patrick's door closing firmly on the floor above made her suddenly conscious of how tired she was after the long day.

As she prepared for bed, she gave herself a mental lecture. Whatever had possessed her to hang around like a beggar waiting for a handout! How fortunate that she'd be asleep and not up and around when Patrick left in the morning. Better still that she didn't number any men like him among her masculine acquaintances in New York. He was the type who made women abandon their resolves and principles without even struggling.

After a half-hour of trying to get to sleep with only a tumbled bed and a nagging headache to show for it, she got up again to take an aspirin.

Another side effect of Mr. Donovan's, she reflected bitterly as she padded back to bed, knowing for a certainty that he was sleeping soundly on the floor above.

4

Carly determined that there was one good thing to be said for Alaska when she got out of bed and went over to open the bedroom drapes the next morning. The weather, at least, was still clear and untroubled. A pale sun was shining on the windswept city street outside her window, and the cluster of fleecy clouds overhead looked as if they'd been put in the vast expanse of sky just for scenic effect.

There was an almost eerie silence in the house and she wasn't surprised to discover the duplicate set of car keys still on the hall table when she made her way to the kitchen. There was also a short note, which caused her to catch her breath momentarily until she read the terse words. "Will arrange to have the window repaired today. Okay?" Patrick's initials were scrawled at the bottom.

Not an epistle to be wrapped in red ribbons and preserved for posterity, Carly decided, and then she resolutely chose to think of more cheerful things.

By the time she'd showered, dressed, and had her breakfast, her spirits were measurably better. When she drank a second cup of coffee, she was keeping company with the nice middle-aged man who arrived to replace the kitchen window. He didn't ask questions about how it came to be broken, but instead spent his time telling Carly of all the things that a visitor to Fairbanks should see. Tops on his list was the civic center called Alaskaland, with a river stern-wheeler and replicas of pioneer houses. Not as much fun as a wilderness camp, Carly thought, before she remembered that she was going to make the best of things. When the glazier finished and she walked out on the porch with him, she discovered that Patrick's car had been parked on the street facing the gallery entrance.

After that, Carly decided there was no reason to linger in the house. She found a cotton sweater to wear in case the breeze freshened, and carefully tucked the house key in her purse after picking up the car keys from the table.

The black leather interior of Patrick's car brought back disturbing memories of his tall figure behind the steering wheel. Carly lingered long enough to run her fingers lightly along the back of the seat. Then she frowned and put her purse and sweater on the passenger side before getting in and starting the car.

She drove first to the picturesque log cabin on the bank of the Chena River which housed the city's Chamber of Commerce tourist-information office. A little later she emerged with an armful of pamphlets which answered every question a tourist might possibly have. In addition, the helpful girl behind the counter had given her an excellent map of the city to make driving easier.

Carly studied it for a moment and then decided to detour by the airport and cancel the flight she'd originally chosen for her departure. After that, she'd head for Alaskaland and investigate the sketching possibilities.

She got on the road to the international airport after only one wrong turn, and fifteen minutes later she pulled into the airport parking lot where Patrick had led her the day before.

There was the usual congestion near the passenger-loading area, so she chose a more deserted section out of deference to Patrick's shining car fenders. There was a rueful smile on her lips as she got out of the car and surveyed them. So far, so good. At least he wouldn't have any complaints on that score.

It didn't take long to transact her business with the airline ticket agent. Then, on an impulse, she inquired about flights to Nome with connections to Anchorage. If Nancy was going to be away long, it might be easiest if the mountain went to Muhammad. At least that way the mountain wouldn't be still sitting around in lonely feminine splendor when Patrick Donovan came back to town.

She was thinking about that depressing circumstance as she walked toward the terminal entrance, until a man's voice called, "Miss Marshall," and she turned in surprise. Craig Norbert, resplendent in a blue copilot's uniform, was coming toward her.

"I thought it was you," he said. "How are you liking Fairbanks by now?"

"Fine, thanks. You look very official today. Are you coming or going?" she asked, mainly for something to say.

"Going. I have a flight for Anchorage in forty-five minutes. Laila and I noticed you last night—when you and Donovan were lurking in the shadows trying to avoid us."

Carly burst out laughing. "I was just as surprised as

you were, Mr. Norbert. Believe it or not, I don't make a career of playing hide and seek."

"I think we were both innocent bystanders," he confirmed, grinning. "Look, I have time for a quick cup of coffee—will you join me?" He gestured toward a stand-up snack bar at the side of the room.

She hesitated for just an instant before she nodded. There was no better way to dispel the lingering memory of Patrick Donovan than to put another man in his place. When that man was attractive and ostensibly pleased to be in her company, why on earth should she resist?

As she walked to the coffee bar with him, she was amused to see the number of feminine glances he attracted. Apparently a well-fitting pilot's uniform was still as effective as ever.

She waited until they both had gotten their coffee before she said, "I'm sorry I didn't get a chance to meet Laila last night."

"Before she took off for the interior this morning with Donovan?" Craig's dark eyes gleamed with amusement. "She was curious about you, too. Especially after Wally's description and discovering that her boss had broken a date to take you out."

"Mr. Donovan was just being polite. My sister is out of town and he knew that I had extra time on my hands."

"And here I am on my way out of town at the wrong time." Craig Norbert looked suitably annoyed. "Just my luck! Laila didn't say how long you were staying in Fairbanks," he added. "Any chance that you'll still be here in three weeks?"

"I doubt it." Carly could have given him a definite negative, having discovered that Alaska had more dangers than the wildlife advertised on the travel posters. She took another sip of coffee. "Just long enough to admire the scenery and buy some souvenirs."

"Most women who visit like to take home gold nuggets for souvenirs. Is that what you have in mind?"

She laughed again. "Hardly. Besides, Wally told me that somebody made off with the best nuggets from the Gold Exchange last week. That gives me an excuse to settle for something smaller."

"You'll find plenty of nuggets around town if you really want to buy some. Wally gets his facts wrong a lot of the time, but it doesn't keep him from airing his opinions."

"So you know him, too? I didn't realize that Fairbanks was such a small town. Or is it because pilots all stick together?"

"Hardly. Wally's strictly a helicopter man and I cross my fingers every time I get in one of those whirlybirds. I only met him through Laila. Most of Donovan's crew are pretty matey. You get to know one, and it ends up like a family gathering. Damned if I can see the attraction myself. Donovan can be a pretty cold fish—even Laila admitted that last night." Craig swirled his coffee absently. "What was your verdict?"

"I'll have to duck that," Carly said diplomatically. "After all, I hardly know the man—except that he's my sister's landlord."

"So I understand." Craig swallowed the last of his coffee.

Carly followed suit and put her cup back on the counter. "Thank you for the coffee. I hope you have a good flight."

"I wish you were going along." He lingered a moment longer. "Layovers are a lot more fun if there's a friendly face around."

"You won't have any trouble finding one. Alaska's a very friendly place. They told me so at the Chamber of Commerce this morning."

He brought his hand up to his visored uniform cap in a mock salute. "At least, next time we meet we'll qualify as old friends. I'll check when I get back in town to find where you are. We have an early-warning system that puts the official one to shame. See you, Carly Marshall."

Carly's intrigued glance wasn't the only one to follow his trim figure through the doorway marked "Official Personnel Only." Craig Norbert walked like a man who knew exactly where he was going and was supremely confident of getting there. His confidence infiltrated his social life too—even a few minutes with him proved that. If he kept an address book, it probably bulged with names and numbers. Quite different from Patrick Donovan, who wouldn't bother to write down a woman's telephone number. He'd expect *her* to call him.

She shook off that depressing thought and went out to the parking lot and unlocked the car. If Alaskaland was all the Chamber of Commerce claimed, it could be the diversion she needed.

Unfortunately, the old river steamboat and historical buildings had a hard time competing. Carly was alone at the civic attraction except for an elderly man who was sweeping a sidewalk close to where she parked the car. She nodded pleasantly as she passed, headed for the restored riverboat *Nenana*, which was the star exhibit.

After she looked it over, she perched on a concrete barrier and pulled out her small sketch pad. The unusual lines of the vessel would be good for her reference files, if nothing else. When she finished, she wandered on through the deserted but sunny streets. She lingered once more to sketch the Gold Rush village and the restored Palace saloon with its worn swinging doors, which must have seen plenty of action on Saturday nights.

She walked on, reading the sign indicating an animal compound beyond, but stubbornly tucked the sketch pad back in her purse at that point. On her second day in Alaska, she wasn't going to seek the tame environs of a zoo. Not while there was still a chance of seeing the real thing in the wilderness. She might not visit Patrick's precious camp, but she could drive to Mt. McKinley National Park later on. The girl at the Chamber of Commerce had practically promised that Dall sheep and moose would be on view there.

Carly became aware of another yearning just then and realized that lunchtime was overdue. She decided to try a restaurant rather than fix a sandwich at home. It would be nice to see people, even if she didn't know anyone to talk to.

She drove back to the center of town and parked near a promising lunch counter combined with a bakery. Unfortunately the friendly chatter around her seemed to increase her feeling of loneliness as she ate. How was it, she wondered, that she could be perfectly self-sufficient for months at a time in Manhattan? Then, overnight, she was casting about for a glimpse of a tall dark-haired man who had put her out of his mind before he'd left the Fairbanks city limits. "Damn," she said softly to herself. "Damn! Damn! Damn!" and then felt like a fool when the passing waitress gave her a wary look.

A visit to a supermarket added a touch of normalcy to the rest of the afternoon, and she felt that she was beginning to behave more like a resident than a tourist when she paid the bill without wincing perceptibly.

By then it was too late to drive out for another look at the pipeline or sketch the big gold dredge, so she contented herself with a quick visit to the Gold Exchange she'd heard so much about.

"I'm really just looking now," she told the man who got up from his desk as she opened the heavy shop door. "It would be nice to buy a tiny gold nugget for my charm bracelet when I go back home. Do you have anything suitable?"

"Our selection's pretty limited right now," he admitted, putting his cigar in an ashtray on the counter before walking to the big old-fashioned safe which stood against the wall. "A lot more limited than usual."

"I heard about the robbery," she replied. "As a matter of fact, I wasn't sure that you'd be open for business."

"We're still breathing—but just barely." The bald-headed man opened one side of the safe and pulled out a tray which he brought back to the counter. "Whoever it was only had time to rip off our office safe, but it sure dented our assets. Even without that, our nugget selection isn't great at this time of year." He put down the tray of oddly shaped nuggets in front of her and flicked through them with a careless finger. "There's not much in the jewelry line now."

"What does the time of year have to do with it?" Carly asked, puzzled.

"The summer prospecting has just started. By fall, the fellows will be bringing in what they find to sell to us." He stirred the trayful of nuggets with his thick finger again. "This stuff has too much quartz in it to be showy. Of course, you might find something in one of the other stores, but I doubt it."

"I see." Carly breathed a soft sigh of disappointment. Although it would have been extravagance to buy a nugget, she was disappointed to find such a limited shopping selection. "Maybe my sister can buy one for me in the fall. She lives in Fairbanks."

The man nodded. "You'll do better that way. Have her come by in August and we'll find something nice for you."

"Thanks, I will. I hope that the police recover your stolen goods," Carly said, lingering in the doorway.

"I won't hold my breath." The man paused while replacing the tray in the safe. "But you can damn well bet nobody's going to pull off another robbery. From now on I'm leaving my Doberman here at night. If he's on guard, I'd think twice about opening the door myself."

There was still a long evening left when Carly arrived back at the house. Although it was nearing dinnertime, it was still bright daylight. If nothing better presented itself, she could stay up till eleven and watch the sunset, she decided, remembering the gorgeous pink and orange rays that had covered the entire western sky the night before.

She had hopes that the phone might ring while she broiled a hamburger and made a salad for dinner. There was always the slight chance that Nancy would call and say "Come and join me in Nome" or "Sorry to have left you in the lurch—I'll be back in Fairbanks on the early plane tomorrow."

But the phone remained stubbornly silent even after Carly had tidied the kitchen and wandered through the section of the house where Nancy had the gallery. There was a well-chosen display of Eskimo craft work with items of scrimshaw and baleen, as well as the more conventional soapstone pieces. Carly was admiring an attractive carving of an Eskimo hunter in a kayak holding a diminutive ivory spear in his upraised hand when she thought she heard the peal of the telephone.

She listened for another ring to make sure before making a dash for it, and was breathless when she snatched up the receiver after running from the front of the gallery. "Hello . . . hello . . ." She had to clear her throat before she could get the second word out.

"Did I find you in the middle of town?" It was an

amused male voice, but not the one that Carly had unconsciously expected to hear.

"No, I was in the gallery," she started to reply before breaking off. "Who _is_ this?"

"Wally. Wally Burton." The helicopter pilot sounded a trifle dashed. "I hope I didn't call at an inconvenient time," he added more stiffly.

"Not at all. As a matter of fact, I thought I might hear from my sister. Certainly not from you," Carly went on, still puzzled. "I didn't know they had telephones out at base camps."

His laughter came over the wire. "Believe me, lady . . . they don't. We have some conveniences, but that's not one of them. I'm back in civilization with an invitation for you."

"I've already had dinner. . . ."

"The invitation's not for tonight." He sounded a little impatient. "This is for tomorrow. Pat said it was okay with him if you still wanted to visit camp."

"Do you mean it? You're not spoofing?"

"Pat would have my hide if I started dealing out invitations to camp without his permission. It's the real thing, all right."

"I wonder what made him change his mind?"

"It was Hal, I imagine. He made a quick trip into camp today and probably reminded the boss that it wasn't polite to leave Nancy's sister cooling her heels in town. If we weren't so busy, he would have been in with the invitation himself."

"Oh, I see." Carly was considerably more subdued, feeling like an unwanted relative being parceled out to unwilling hosts. "Really, this isn't necessary. I'm perfectly fine here in town. You can tell Pat—"

"Nuh-uh. _You_ come and tell him," Wally interrupted. "My orders were to bring you in, and that's what I do."

"You sound like one of those Canadian Mounties in

an old-time movie," she told him with some irony. "Only you have the plot mixed—they went after the villain, not the girl."

"Not in the movies I saw," Wally informed her. He lowered his voice suggestively. "Will you come willingly, ma'am . . . or do I have to use force?"

"You're crazy!"

"I don't know why you say that. They had that line in a TV western last week and the sheriff got the horse as well as the girl. Besides, I thought you wanted to see our camp."

"I do."

"Then what are you stalling for?" he asked with some logic. "We can't offer you a horse to ride off into the sunset, but you can have a helicopter ride first thing in the morning."

"You really mean it!"

"Lady, you're hard to convince. Of course I do. How did you think you'd get there? That four-lane freeway in town doesn't go far beyond the city limits. Probably that's why Pat decided you should see what Alaska is really like."

By then Carly was past worrying about her pride, but she did have another question. "Is Laila going to be there, too?"

"I suppose so. Unless Pat sends her back to town. I wouldn't count on it, though," Wally added. "Probably he's decided she can chaperon you. That way, nobody can say anything."

"I just wondered . . ."

"Uh-huh." He wasn't convinced. "Don't worry, Laila's okay if she doesn't think you're interested in Pat. She staked a claim in that direction right off."

"She has nothing whatsoever to worry about." Carly's proclamation was weakened when she added, "I'd think Pat would have something to say about it."

"Never fear—but we don't discuss it in the helicopter at five hundred feet. That reminds me, I hope you don't mind driving down to Ophir Junction in the morning. There's a good road all the way, and it would be more convenient if I can fly in and get you there."

"Of course." Carly made a resolve to go and find a road map as soon as she hung up. "Where do I meet you in Ophir?"

"There's an airport at the edge of town."

"Only one?"

"You won't have any trouble locating it. The whole place consists of a general store, laundromat, and gas station."

Carly bit her lip, wishing that she'd manage one sentence without putting her foot in her mouth. "Fair enough," she said. "What time?"

"Around nine. I should be back in camp to pick up Pat afterward. You'll have to leave Fairbanks by seven, if that's okay."

"Not just okay—it's wonderful!" Carly exclaimed, making no effort to hide her delight.

"Pat said to keep your luggage light. Even Laila just changes one khaki shirt for another when she's in the field."

"I don't have anything like that to wear." Carly tried to think what was in her wardrobe that would fit the circumstances. "Would T-shirts be okay?"

"Only if you wear a long-sleeved jacket on top of them. That's rough country. Hiking shoes and jeans will do for the rest. Look, I have to hang up now. You figure it out. The store at Ophir could fit you out in the morning if you're desperate."

She could sense his impatience so she didn't prolong the discussion. "All right. I'll see you in the morning. And, Wally . . ."

"Yes?"

"Thanks very much."

"Don't thank me. Save it for Pat. You might just be the one to soften him up."

After that cryptic remark, she heard his receiver go down. She was grinning like a cat who's just heard movement at the nearest mouse hole when she replaced her own. Afterward she floated to the hallway in a delighted daze and sat down on the bottom stair step to think things over.

There wasn't any time to waste, she told herself sternly, even as she wondered what had really prompted Patrick's abrupt about-face. Whatever it was, she'd have to be cool and polite when she arrived, not giving him or the efficient Laila cause for complaint.

First off, she'd check the glove compartment in the car and look for a map that showed how to get to Ophir Junction. If there wasn't one, she'd have to find a service station to supply one right away. There wouldn't be many stations open at the crack of dawn when she planned to leave, and she wasn't going to risk being late at the airfield.

Once that problem was settled, she could pack. It was a pity that her vacation wardrobe was more suited to the South Seas than Alaska. The best she could do was a pair of jeans topped with T-shirts or a cotton blouse and a poplin jacket. Probably it wouldn't hurt to throw in a cardigan sweater, as well. Canvas shoes would have to do instead of hiking shoes. At least a helicopter ride wouldn't require anything special, and she could sketch animals around camp without needing more rugged gear.

It was late when she finally got to bed, but by then her sketching materials were packed on top of her overnight case and it was placed by the kitchen door—ready to be put in the trunk of the car without wasted motion. The road map had shown that Ophir Junction was a good two-hour drive from Fairbanks, so Carly set her travel alarm for five o'clock. If she arrived early at the airport, she could always catnap in the car until the helicopter arrived.

Unfortunately sleep remained stubbornly elusive— probably because she lay tense, worrying whether she'd sleep through the alarm when it was time to go off. Then, as the hours passed, she worried because she'd look like a zombie on the one day when it mattered.

When the alarm finally did sound, she had fallen into an uneasy sleep just two hours before. A quick look in the bathroom mirror as she headed for a hasty shower revealed her pale countenance, and she muttered in annoyance. Probably Laila was a woman who managed helicopter rides and trips to wilderness camps without losing a wink of sleep. Carly stepped under tepid water, and then, bracing herself, turned the spray to cold.

It took six months off her life, but when she climbed into her clothes and went down to a breakfast of cold cereal and coffee, she was wide-awake and could have balanced a checkbook.

Instead, she pored over the road map again while her coffee cooled. Once she got out of Fairbanks, it was simply a case of staying on the marked route. She didn't have to worry about driving in the dark; it was daylight outside despite the early hour.

Five minutes later, she'd washed the breakfast dishes and stored them neatly away. If Nancy did return home unexpectedly, it would be to a tidy kitchen. Carly wondered if she should leave a note for her sister and then decided against it. Hal would keep his fiancée informed.

Carly's pulse beat faster than usual until she found the right road out of town. Once past the city limits on the main highway to the southeast, she settled back in the seat of Patrick's car and kept the accelerator steadily on the speed limit.

It was easy to do at that time of the morning because the two-lane road was practically deserted except for the occasional pickup trucks that whizzed by her, whose drivers showed a complete disregard for the posted limit. Carly hoped they were familiar with the road, because dips in the surface caused by permafrost made driving unexpectedly hazardous even at a lower speed.

She did let her gaze wander over the magnificent snow-covered peaks of the Alaska Range in front of the windshield. The craggy sides that were still in shade were bluish-purple, but their icy tops glistened brightly in the sun against a vibrant blue sky.

The view was breathtaking on such a crystal-clear morning and would have made Carly's heart beat faster even if she hadn't been speculating what else she'd find in that mountain range, aside from natural wonders. The base camp must be somewhere in that general direction, tucked among the stunted black spruce trees which seemed to be everywhere. There were occasional clumps of birch and aspen which quaked obediently to legend in the breeze, which grew stronger with every mile.

Carly's steady driving brought her to the outskirts of Ophir Junction even earlier than she'd planned. She had driven the last ten miles amused and intrigued after seeing signs at the roadside proclaiming a "Bear Drop Zone" and "Tank Crossing." Fortunately she reached the junction without sighting either obstacle, and she resolved to ask Wally for an explanation when there was time.

She decided it was a good thing she was inside the speed limit because Ophir was so small she would have driven right past if she hadn't been paying attention. There was a dusty and modest sign with an arrow indicating the town airport just before the sprawling general store that Wally had mentioned. Carly braked and pulled off onto the graveled area in front of it faster than she'd planned, fishtailing on the loose surface before she finally pulled up in front of the store.

She sighed with relief as she turned off the ignition, thankful that there hadn't been any spectators to her arrival. As she got out of the car and went to inspect the entrance of the general store, she soon discovered the reason why. Even though it was the sum total of Ophir's commercial enterprise, the store kept hours only from eight-thirty to six. Carly glanced at her watch and frowned as she saw it was barely seven o'clock.

Why on earth hadn't she considered that she'd arrive before anything was open? All during the drive she'd thought about a second breakfast at the end of it, and now it seemed that all she was going to get was plenty of fresh air.

She scuffed her shoe in the gravel, annoyed that she hadn't planned to bring a thermos and some food with her. That was the trouble with being used to a coffee shop on each corner. Ophir Junction didn't even have four corners; it had one grocery store with three gas pumps and one coin laundry. The last discovery was made as she peered around the side of the store.

She walked over and inspected the coin washing machine and drier. If she'd really been efficient, she would have brought her laundry and put the spare time to good use.

She yawned as she thought about it. Now that the drive was over and she could relax, her lack of sleep was making itself felt. It was a temptation to drive out to the airfield and curl up on the front seat of the car while she waited for Wally to arrive. Then she decided it would be even better to walk the block or two back to the airport turnoff. The exercise would be good for her and it would be something to do in the interim. By the time she walked down and back, someone might have arrived to unlock the store and put on some coffee at the snack bar which was advertised along with the grocery specials.

The leisurely walk to the turnoff wasn't unpleasant therapy. Since there was scarcely any traffic at that early hour, she was able to walk on the edge of the hard-surfaced highway rather than the dusty gravel shoulder. Unfortunately the access road to the airfield was simply a narrow trail of packed earth which cut through the scrub spruce trees. Carly bit her lip as she heard the whine of a mosquito around her head, and then relaxed as that warning signal gave way to the buzzing of a fly. A big fly, she discovered as she batted it away from her face, bigger than anything she'd seen at home. Of course her insect repellent was in her suitcase, locked safely in the trunk of the car.

She was so preoccupied with the horsefly that it wasn't until a moment later she realized the buzzing sound had grown all out of proportion. Puzzled, she stepped out from under the overhang of the trees and felt excitement rise within her when she saw a helicopter approaching the far end of the tiny airstrip.

How ridiculous that she hadn't considered Wally might be early, too! She hesitated on the edge of the track, wondering whether she should hurry back to get the car or walk on down and tell him she was raring to go!

While she was still trying to decide, the bright orange copter advanced steadily toward the middle of the airstrip. Belatedly, it occurred to Carly that she had no reason to conclude it *was* Wally. Whoever the pilot was, he was taking his time and hovering carefully before setting the whirlybird down.

As Carly stood watching, she noted an ancient

lean-to hut at the edge of the runway, close to the place the pilot had chosen for his landing pad. The small building apparently served a twofold purpose: it was a shelter of sorts and provided a base for the tattered windsock on the roof. An instant later her gaze fastened on an unfamiliar station wagon parked under the trees near the shed.

She was glad then that she hadn't scurried up to proclaim her presence. Probably it wasn't Wally in the helicopter at all. Or if it was, he wasn't alone. She discerned that as the copter settled onto the pad, raising a storm of dust with its powerful rotor blades.

A second man was sitting in the passenger seat, and she only had a glimpse of his profile before the helicopter turned in landing and Wally's face came into view. His mop of long fair hair was curtained by the billed cap he'd worn in Fairbanks, but that was the only familiar feature. Instead of the cheerful mien he'd displayed in town, his expression was grim and purposeful.

Carly moved instinctively into the protection of the spruce grove as she watched the men discussing something inside the Plexiglas bubble of the copter, while the rotor blades continued to turn. Then the man in the passenger seat shoved open the door on his side and got out, carrying an attaché case at his side.

Wally barely allowed him time to reach the parked station wagon before he secured the door and took off with the helicopter again, its high-thrust engine tearing a rent in the quiet Alaskan air.

Carly's lips parted in amazement as she followed the progress of the vivid orange craft back toward the Alaska range, wondering if she'd suddenly lost her reason. It had never occurred to her that Wally wouldn't pick her up as arranged.

The revving of a car engine came then, segueing into the copter's noise like an orchestrated arrangement. Carly stayed behind the trees as Wally's passenger reversed the parked car and drove rapidly along the track toward her. He was alongside only for an instant, but that was enough for her to let out another gasp of surprise as she recognized Craig Norbert's intent face. She remained unmoving as the station wagon sped on to the main road, slowing just a trifle in the turn before disappearing in the direction of Fairbanks.

Carly thrust her hands in the pockets of her jeans and walked out to the track. She started back toward the highway herself, knowing there was no need to worry about concealment any longer. At the rate Craig was driving, he'd be in the next borough before she got back to the store.

She scuffed her shoes carelessly in the dirt, more concerned with what she'd just seen than paying attention to what she was doing. Why in the dickens had Wally left without picking her up? What was more to the point—why was Craig Norbert riding around in one of Patrick's helicopters instead of doing his own job? When she'd seen him the day before, he'd been practically on his way to Anchorage. Supposedly out of town for weeks. He either had a quick turnaround, she mused, or he hadn't made his flight in the first place.

Of course she could ask what was going on when she saw Wally again, but the unannounced arrival, the tense looks on the men's faces, and the speedy departure of both the helicopter and the car made her leery of getting involved.

Her attention was diverted by a squirrel scurrying across the track in front of her, dodging into the safety of the trees. She smiled at the last impudent flick of his tail and then her expression sobered as her thoughts came back to the strange goings-on. There was no use fussing about it, she reasoned. It was like being on a treadmill—she could go on and on without getting anywhere.

With any luck, the Ophir storekeeper might have come to work early and put the coffeepot on. And later, Wally might arrive with a perfectly simple explanation. There was no reason to look for trouble, Carly told herself. Intelligent people didn't go around creating problems when there were none.

But when she arrived back at the car, the store was still closed and there wasn't a whiff of coffee in the breeze which stirred the dust outside the padlocked door.

Carly leaned disconsolately against the radiator grille of Patrick's car, suspecting that the other omens were going to be just as unassailable. She glanced at her wristwatch and shook her head. Unassailable, and, from the looks of things, a long time in coming.

5

It was exactly nine o'clock when Carly caught her second glimpse of the bright orange helicopter. This time, she was standing beside Patrick's car, which she had intentionally parked in a prominent place at the landing strip, away from the spot where Craig had left his transportation. By then she had decided to remain discreetly silent about what she'd observed earlier, unless Wally mentioned it.

A tremor of excitement passed through her as she watched the helicopter settle down again—almost in the exact location that Wally had chosen before. This time, however, he cut his switches after landing and the rotor blades came to a graceful stop. Like an outsized ceiling fan, Carly thought irrelevantly, as she moved out onto the runway.

Wally opened the door of the Plexiglas bubble and jumped lithely to the ground, pulling off his cap as he came to greet her. "Top of the morning," he called.

"No wonder Pat wanted you to come calling. Imagine finding a woman who can be on time!"

He was smiling as he came up to her, but Carly's attention was caught by the puffy bruises on his cheek and jaw. "What in the world happened to you?" she asked, too startled to be polite.

"It's nothing." He shrugged carelessly. "I got into a little argument, that's all. Unfortunately, the other guy was bigger than I was. I'm practically back to normal by now," he continued with a twisted grin. "Tonight I can eat steak instead of having it draped over my eye."

"At least you weren't hurt in your line of work."

"Don't be silly." Wally waved a hand toward the helicopter behind him. "Betsy here is dependable and a perfect lady—provided you handle her gently." His glance swept around Carly's figure. "Where's your stuff?"

"Behind the building. I'll get it." She turned to ask, "Should I leave Mr. Donovan's car parked over there?"

"Sure thing. Somebody'll probably be in later today and drive it back to town." Wally walked beside her to pick up her bag. "You're traveling pretty light."

"There's no point in buying a new wardrobe for a day or so. Besides, hiking shoes aren't practical for walking to work on Fifth Avenue."

"You mean that's all you have?" Wally frowned as he stared down at her low canvas shoes.

"There are some sandals and bedroom slippers in Fairbanks, but I didn't think I'd need them. All I plan to do is some sketching around your camp," she added defensively.

He still looked skeptical but he said, "Laila probably has some extra stuff if you run short," before leading the way back to the helicopter and putting her overnight bag behind the seats. He turned then to help her in. "Put your foot on that step and I'll hoist you up."

"I can make it." Carly tried to sound as if crawling into a helicopter was second nature, and then spoiled the effect by asking, "Where do I sit?"

"Right there." He grinned and shoved his cap on the back of his head. "Since you're a guest, I'll let you ride beside me. There are a couple of geologists that don't rate so high."

"What do you make them do—straddle the tail?" She kept her voice light, ignoring the way her stomach muscles tightened as the moment of takeoff approached.

"That's an idea I hadn't thought of." He went around and vaulted easily onto the seat beside her. "Next time I'll keep their rock samples up here with me and send the men packing. Fasten your seat belt, honey. If I don't get back pretty soon, Pat will be radioing Fairbanks for a new pilot."

Carly pulled the belt across her lap and fumbled with the catch. "Just like an airplane so far."

"Lady, that's heresy! Don't compare my Betsy to one of those fixed-wing jobs—no way."

"I meant the seat belt . . ." She broke off as she saw his teasing grin. "All right, so I'm nervous. I don't even like takeoffs on 747's."

"Wait until you've been up a few times in a whirlybird. The trouble is that you've been watching those television movies where the copter drops like a rock in the last reel, taking the villain along. Isn't that right?" He laughed at her guilty expression. "I thought so. Well, you can relax. If there's a mechanical malfunction in Betsy, we can glide down as neat as anything."

"You mean I don't have to worry about . . ." She made a graphic downward gesture.

"Not unless you distract me and we fly into the side

of a mountain," he said cheerfully. "But even a parachute wouldn't help then."

"I promise to keep as quiet as a mouse."

"Okay, then I'll give you the rundown so you'll know what's going on. These are your headphones," he said, indicating a pair on the bench seat between them. "Put them on so you can hear me during the flight. If you want to talk, just push the red button on the cord. Okay?" He waited for her nod, and went on briskly. "This horizontal lever over here at my left is the collective, and this thing in front is called a cyclic—"

"I thought they were called a stick."

"That's in fixed-wing aircraft, not helicopters." He shot a sideways glance at her bewildered face and leaned forward to place the throttle in cutoff position before turning on the ignition key. "Look, Carly, just trust me. We'll give the treetops and mountains a wide berth." He grinned impudently. "Pat would hate to have this expensive baby bent before he'd finished paying for it."

With that reassurance, Carly had to be content. The vertical instrument panel between their seats looked complicated, but Wally's fingers moved surely over the switches on his preflight testing. There had been a whirring sound when he'd turned the ignition switch, much like the starter on a car. Then a ticking—again like the spark plug functioning on a combustion engine—before he'd twisted the grip throttle on what he'd called the collective. Then the noise became loud and high-pitched, forcing her to hurriedly don her headphones. Wally continued to watch the turbine speed indicator on the instrument panel until, with all warning lights out, he twisted the throttle to full open position and Betsy rose smoothly. Carly showed a greater reaction; she drew in her breath sharply as they angled upward over the trees, feeling as if she'd gone up in an express elevator.

The visibility from the helicopter was magnificent, but there was a strange feeling of being pitched on her nose when Wally evidently reached his cruising height and Betsy was urged forward.

"What's the matter?" Wally asked cheerfully through the headphones. Then, when she shot him a worried look, he added, "It's okay. Not a mountain in sight, and around here we don't worry about midair collisions. Now, push your red button and tell me if you're okay."

"I'm fine," she said after doing as instructed, "except that I feel as if I'm wearing shoes with heels that are too high."

"Occupational hazard in helicopters. At least it's easy to look down. How do you like the view?"

Carly took a firm grip on the bench and forced herself to look at the unending spruce forest beneath them as they sped along. The mountains she had worried about were still a comfortable distance away, their snowy peaks glinting in the sun. Then she realized that the helicopter was rocking in the gusts of wind. The motion, combined with staring downward through the bubble, made her queasy and she straightened in a hurry.

"What's the matter?" Wally wanted to know, noting her uneasy expression.

"I know this sounds silly but . . ."—she swallowed with an effort—"does anybody ever get seasick in a helicopter?"

"Oh, Lord, is the motion bothering you?" He went on without waiting for her to answer. "Keep your head up. You can look at the scenery another time. It's this damned wind today. Most of the time it isn't bumpy at this season."

"*Now* he tells me." Wally looked so concerned that

Carly decided she simply couldn't be sick. It was going to be a triumph of mind over matter if she could possibly manage. "How high are we?" she asked, mainly for something to take her mind off the motion.

"About five hundred feet." His reply came promptly. "We go down a hundred feet on survey trips, but it's safer at this elevation." Seeing her raised eyebrows, he added, "Gives me a chance to pick out a nice soft spot if there's one of those mechanical malfunctions."

"Let's not talk about it," she put in hastily. "My stomach's just settling down again. How much longer before we get there?"

"About fifteen more minutes to base camp. After that, it's up to Pat."

"I don't understand," she faltered. "What does he have to do with it?"

"Just about everything. He runs the company, remember. I don't know whether he plans to have you stay at the base or out at a fly camp."

"What's a fly camp?" she wanted to know, recalling the energetic horsefly she'd encountered earlier by the airstrip. If Pat Donovan was intent on revenge, that would be setting about it in the right way.

Her shudder made Wally's grin broaden. "You have the wrong idea. Fly camp isn't 'fly' as in bugs— it's 'fly' as in whirlybirds. That's the name we use for temporary locations. Where we have all of the inconveniences and very few home comforts."

"Does Mr. Donovan ever stay at a fly camp?" There was suspicion in her voice.

"All during the season," Wally said, sounding surprised. "The rest of the time, I drop him off in places that make *my* stomach do flip-flops. I've put him on ridges so sharp that there's no place to land—he climbs down on Betsy's skids and gets off that way. You

wouldn't catch me doing it. Not for any salary check."

Carly looked at the deep ravines visible on the Alaska range, which was looming closer, and bit her lip. "I'm beginning to think that everybody in this state is a little bit crazy."

"It helps," Wally agreed cheerfully. "See the lake over there to the left? We have a fly camp just on the other side of that hill behind it."

"The water looks beautiful," she said, forgetting about the motion of the helicopter as she admired the deep blue of the mountain lake. "Are there cabins around it?"

"There's a beaver colony on the south rim, but they have a waiting list. We stay at an abandoned trapper's cabin up at the other end. There's a nice view but the roof leaks, which doesn't help the market value."

She started to giggle. "I get the idea."

"It takes a while for you out-of-state types," he said, "but you'll find out soon enough. Don't forget to give way in this part of the world if a grizzly argues about territorial rights."

"Much more advice like that and I won't even get out of the helicopter."

"I *told* you that you'd learn to love it," he replied, deliberately misunderstanding. "See the smoke over there?" He pointed toward a small settlement beside a winding stream a mile or so ahead of them.

"Base camp?"

"Uh-huh." He shoved his throttle grip slightly forward and started a gradual descent. Carly peered beyond the instrument panel at the physical layout of the camp. There appeared to be five regulation tent houses and one larger structure where the smoke originated.

"The cookhouse?" she asked hopefully.

"Right." Wally was bringing the helicopter steadily down on a grassy patch near the curving stream.

"Does that smoke mean they're still serving breakfast?"

"Either that or Patrick is simmering because I'm so late." Wally brought Betsy down to the grass, settling onto the left skid momentarily before the touchdown was complete. "There we are—still in one piece," he said, cutting the ignition switches and turning to smile at her. "Now, aren't you sorry that you wasted all that energy worrying?"

His nonsense made her forget to ask why Patrick would think they were late. They had left Ophir almost dead on time.

"I'll bet that your knuckles won't be as white next time." Wally was grinning at her like a father whose offspring had performed beyond all expectations.

Carly glanced down at her hands to discover she was still clutching the edge of her seat. She flushed under his amused regard and unfastened her safety belt. "I hoped that I looked nonchalant," she said ruefully.

"At least your teeth didn't chatter . . ." He broke off as he spotted a man and woman coming toward them. "Here's the welcoming committee." Then, after another glance at the tall man striding alongside an attractive brunette dressed in khaki pants and shirt, Wally said, "I don't like that expression on Pat's face."

Carly was wondering if she'd been safer at five hundred feet, after all. "Are you sure that I'm invited?"

Wally didn't have a chance to reply, as the helicopter door was pulled open just then and Patrick greeted Wally with, "I was about to radio for another copter. Where in the hell have you been!"

"We did a little sightseeing," the pilot said easily,

not particularly upset. "Sorry if we loused up the schedule."

"Pat, aren't you going to introduce us?" It was a chiding reminder from the brunette who hovered at his side.

"Sorry . . . Laila Anson, this is Carlyle Marshall."

Carly nodded pleasantly. "I was just wondering what happened to 'Good morning,' 'Nice to see you,' or 'I'm glad you could make it.' " From her seat in the copter she regarded Patrick with a level brown-eyed gaze. "Thank you for sending Wally to pick me up."

Patrick's tanned cheeks turned suspiciously redder after her bland comment. "I'm sorry," he began, and then broke off to say, "I hope you had a good trip."

"My, my," Laila breathed at his side. "That's a switch."

The frown came back to his forehead at her words. "Are you ready to go?" he asked her tersely.

"I have been for some time," Laila reminded him.

Patrick nodded and turned back to Carly. "Allow me," he said, putting two hard hands at her waist.

"Just a minute," Wally interrupted. "We have a little unfinished business." Without any other explanation he caught Carly's chin between his thumb and forefinger, holding her head firmly as he leaned over to kiss her.

She was so surprised that she remained motionless in his clasp at first. But as his lips continued to press relentlessly on hers, she put her palms against his chest and shoved hard.

Wally let her go reluctantly—at least that's how it must have looked to the two observers. What they didn't realize was that the seat of a helicopter wasn't constructed for amorous advances—the designers, not surprisingly, giving other aspects priority.

"Honestly!" Carly emerged from his grasp sputtering angrily. "Whatever do you think—?"

Wally bent to her again, dropping a hasty kiss on her lips. It didn't further his cause, but it did stem her tirade. "Sorry, darling, I didn't mean to embarrass you."

"If you're *quite* finished . . ." Patrick's deep voice was ominous and his hands tightened painfully at Carly's waistline as he swung her to the ground.

Carly was jarred by the impact, and she glared at him. It was bad enough to be pounced on by Wally without getting tossed around like a parcel-post package besides.

"There's coffee in the cook tent if you'd like some," Patrick announced two inches over her head. "I'm sorry that you'll be without company for the moment, but Wally will be back as soon as he drops us off."

The pilot frowned, clearly puzzled by the announcement. "You've changed the schedule. I thought—"

"You can think on your own time," Patrick grated, assisting Laila into the helicopter and then getting in beside her. "Take us back to Ophir first. Laila's driving on to Fairbanks."

"Whatever you say," Wally muttered.

"You're so right," Laila mocked, beaming as she glanced at her employer. "I had no idea I was going to have an escort even partway. Is that to make up for sending me back to town so fast?"

A flicker of resignation—or was it tiredness?—went over Patrick's face. "You're going back to the office because there's work to be done there and you damn well know it."

"Pat, dear, don't be so stuffy." She patted his cheek affectionately.

The caress didn't last long. Patrick moved out of reach abruptly to close the helicopter door.

"Just a minute," Carly said before he could accomplish it. "May I have my bag, please? If it's not too much trouble." Her tone was without expression and the words couldn't be faulted.

Patrick's eyes narrowed ominously but he twisted in the seat to reach the suitcase.

She forestalled him when he would have gotten out of the helicopter to carry it for her. "Thanks, I can manage."

He was reluctant to hand it over, but other than engaging in a tug-of-war, there wasn't anything he could do.

"Here are your car keys," Carly said, handing them up.

"I'll be back in a flash," Wally said. "Before you even have time to get lonely."

"I'm sorry to leave you on your own," Patrick told her in a tone that showed he meant nothing of the kind. "Ordinarily, Wing Loo, our cook, would be around, but he won't be back until later today."

"And even old Toklat's out at a fly camp with Hal," Wally reported.

Patrick didn't look pleased with his interruption. He turned back to Carly and said, "Make yourself at home but *don't* wander around. If anything on four feet comes calling, stay in the mess hall and lock the door. Understand?" He nodded in dismissal and slammed the door of the helicopter without waiting for a reply.

Wally gave her a thumbs-up sign and Laila managed to raise her eyebrows commiseratingly before Carly turned and walked out from under the rotor blades, heading toward the row of tent houses. She reached the door of the big cabin which served as the mess hall before the noise of the helicopter attained takeoff volume. Only then did she turn and wave briefly. She couldn't have told if there was any response because her eyes were blinded with angry tears and she just managed to get safely inside the cookhouse door before they spilled over.

Anger vied with frustration for the next few minutes. She slumped into a nearby canvas chair and let the tears run unchecked down her cheeks. Why had Patrick ever invited her in the first place? He was obviously annoyed at having her underfoot and visibly seethed after Wally kissed her in that ridiculous way.

Remembrance of the incident brought a new wash of tears. There was no use trying to explain that she and Wally hadn't been gamboling around the meadows all morning as Patrick clearly thought. She sniffed and fumbled for a handkerchief as the crest of her emotional onslaught started to recede.

For the first time, she surveyed her surroundings, grateful that she'd been able to do her weeping in private. Then her spirits rose as she discovered a neatly laid tray on a table against the wall. There was a vaccuum bottle containing steaming coffee and a plate of sweet rolls covered with plastic.

Carly blew her nose and tucked her handkerchief back in her pocket. She was still upset from her bout of weeping, but a swallow of the hot coffee helped immeasurably. By the time she'd finished a mammoth homemade cinnamon roll along with it, she felt like a new person. Still frayed around the edges, she decided, but damned if she'd go into a decline because of the arrogant creature who had just left.

After that assessment, she almost convinced herself that she wouldn't even have cried if she hadn't been short on sleep from the night before.

She carried her cup over to a stainless-steel sink mounted in a rough-looking but sturdy counter and turned a faucet. When hot water came out, her eyebrows went up. So this was camping in the wilderness! A furtive peek inside the big refrigerator made her eyebrows go even higher. Apparently Mr. Donovan and his geologists preferred steak on the menu. Every day of the week, if the pile on the shelf in the freezer compartment meant anything. No wonder Laila was anxious to come to base camp; the food alone would make it worthwhile.

Carly's thoughts flickered rebelliously back to Laila's employer at that point, wondering what would happen when they reached Ophir Junction. Probably nothing more intimate than a discussion of rock samplings, if his disposition hadn't improved.

She decided that she wasn't going to let Patrick's whims ruin any more of her day. A little later, she'd come back and fix a sandwich for lunch, but just now she'd inspect the tent houses. She'd put her bag in the one she was to occupy, and unpack her sketching pad. Even if there weren't any animals around, the view of the mountains was fabulous and would provide wonderful material.

When she emerged from the cookhouse, the camp was quiet and peaceful in the sunshine. The Alaskan stillness had bothered Carly at first, but she was gradually getting used to it, and now she could feel her tense muscles relaxing as she looked around her.

The tent houses were neat and functional; sturdy white canvas tops were erected above wooden bases on a section of hard-packed earth. Carly walked to the nearest one and opened the door gingerly, hoping Patrick would approve of her investigation. The antiseptic interior reassured her; two cots with air mattresses constituted the bulk of the furnishings, along with a tent heater. The wooden floor was unadorned except for a sifting of sand which showed the premises hadn't been occupied recently.

That meant she didn't have to look any further, Carly thought thankfully. She deposited her case on the nearest cot and took out her cosmetic kit, along with her sketching materials.

Another glance around the tent's interior showed that indoor plumbing was one refinement still lacking. Carly grimaced and peered outside, discovering two small huts which might provide the answer.

The first was the camp shower house, with rough plumbing and a gas heater so that residents were blessed with hot showers despite their surroundings. Two hand basins were below a mirror at the other side, and Carly shivered as she felt the temperature of the cold water in a faucet there. No doubt where that came from. The stream at the edge of camp must originate up on those snowy mountain slopes.

As she trudged back to her tent house a little later, she was hoping that Patrick would let her stay long enough to accomplish some serious sketching. Certainly the base camp was big enough that she could stay out of his way, and after the morning's greeting, she had no doubt that he would cooperate.

Carly wandered outside the tent after collecting her sketching materials and looked around again. The quiet, crisp air smelled good enough to be bottled and sold by the ounce. Only the buzzing of a fly disrupted the halcyon solitude, and Carly laughed aloud when she discovered it was the common bluebottle variety.

She found a flat rock by the edge of the stream where she could sit and rest her sketch pad on her knee. A quick look showed that there weren't any large four-footed creatures in view, and she turned a professional eye toward the Alaska range spread out before her.

Afterward she was grateful that the grizzlies in the neighborhood kept their distance, because she didn't surface to reality until the whine of an engine finally defeated her concentration. Her glance went to the sky automatically and located Betsy's bright shape winging toward her. But not from Ophir, she deduced, narrowing her eyes thoughtfully. That meant that Patrick must be working somewhere to the north, if her sense of direction was right.

Wally confirmed it for her a few minutes later after he brought the helicopter down on the patch of grass he'd used before. He was out almost before the rotors stopped turning, greeting Carly in his usual breezy manner. "Still in one piece? I told Patrick that no self-respecting bear would dare argue with you so he didn't have to worry. I hope you have lunch ready."

Carly surveyed him warily as she replaced her pencils in a protective plastic pocket. "I'm not concerned with the bears around here half so much as some of the two-legged wolves. What in the dickens were you trying to prove with that . . . that . . . ?" Words failed her as she tried to describe his action.

"Affectionate farewell?" Wally supplied, undaunted. "You know you liked it, honey. What's all the fuss about?"

Carly pulled up on the path. "The fuss, as you call it, is because I don't enjoy charades without being cued in on the action. I know an affectionate farewell and I also know a grandstand play—give me credit for recognizing the difference. If you wanted to impress Laila Anson, there were better ways of going about it. You didn't convince anybody."

Wally had pulled up beside her, and a frown creased his forehead. "You don't think that Laila's . . . ?" There was a slight pause before he cleared his throat and went on. "Well, my playacting must have convinced somebody, because Laila and Pat climbed my frame about it all the way to Ophir. Of course, I didn't get *all* the blame."

"I can believe that," Carly put in drily. "At this rate, it'll be a wonder if your boss even tosses me a crust of bread before inventing an excuse to get rid of me tomorrow. Unless you've dropped him off in the next borough and he won't be back for a week." She gave Wally a hopeful sideways glance.

"Sorry, love. He's just going over the budget figures with Hal at a fly camp. I'm due to pick him up tonight and bring him back here. At least, that was the latest—I'll call him at three and see if plans have changed."

"Call?"

Her puzzled expression clearly amused him. "On the radio. Didn't you see it in the storage tent?"

She shook her head. "I didn't investigate very far. I'm curious about one thing, though. How did you get all this heavy stuff here in the first place? Surely you didn't fly it in by helicopter."

"It would be gold-plated if we did." He shoved his cap farther forward to shade his eyes. "Pat arranged for it to be brought in by bulldozers—on skids when the rivers and stream were still frozen. It isn't cheap that way, but he believes in good working conditions. When the men are out for months during the summer, they like some home comforts. Good food and hot showers make it easier to hire an efficient crew."

"And a good helicopter pilot."

"That, too." Wally knew his ability and wasn't hesitant in acknowledging it. "But make that plural. Pat's other pilot will be along with Wing Loo and a barrel of fuel later this afternoon."

She paused at the door of the mess cabin to ask, "Helicopter fuel?"

"That's right." He pulled open the door and gestured her inside, carefully closing the screen behind them. "We bring a four-hundred-pound barrel of it in a sling beneath us." He grinned over his shoulder as he headed for the refrigerator. "That way, we can dump it fast if we get in trouble. Anything else you want to know?"

"Just one thing." She came up to peer in the refrigerator beside him. "What's for lunch?"

After that, it didn't take long for them to prepare two steaks and slice tomatoes for a salad. Served with buttered French bread and another cup of coffee, it was a remarkably satisfying meal.

Carly volunteered to do the housekeeping chores when they'd finished.

"Better you than me," Wally said, barely hiding a yawn. "I think I'll sneak a nap before I get in touch with Pat. Sure you don't want to keep me company?"

"I don't have anything to say to Mr. Donovan," Carly said, choosing to misunderstand him. She picked up their dishes and started toward the sink. "Thanks just the same."

"That wasn't what I had in mind." Wally grinned unrepentantly. "Okay, have it your way."

"I intend to. You made your points with Laila, so now you can relax."

"Don't you ever? Relax, I mean." Wally lingered by the screen door, twirling his cap on his finger. "Or maybe it's none of my business."

Carly gave him a crooked smile, tired of the conversation but not wanting to antagonize him. "Did anyone ever tell you that you cook a fabulous steak in addition to your other talents?"

"Only Betsy, and I have her well-trained." He paused halfway through the door. "Incidentally, don't wander off. Pat was very firm about keeping you safe."

"This dishpan should be safe enough," she replied, reaching for the liquid soap. "But if you hang around much longer, you're in danger of being snagged by a dish towel."

"Quick takeoffs are my specialty. I'll see you later. And if you want anything in the meantime, holler and I'll come running."

Carly watched through the screen door as he walked, whistling, down the tent row. He turned in at the last one, banging the door carelessly behind him. She shook her head and moved back to the dishpan, thinking it was impossible to remain annoyed with such a character. He committed outrageous acts with abandon and seemed apparently unaffected when his victims rebelled. Patrick had read the riot act all the way to Ophir, but it merely gave Wally a robust appetite for lunch. And after she had thought she'd put him firmly in his place, he was still trying for a low-key flirtation.

Carly rubbed the end of her nose with the back of her soapy hand and succeeded in stifling a sneeze. Fine thing if she was catching cold now! Maybe the sensible thing would be to take a short nap after finishing the dishes, so she'd be rested and able to cope when Patrick returned.

It was a fine theory, even if it didn't work out as she planned. The first part went according to schedule; Carly found the cot and air mattress to be as comfortable as she could hope—especially after she appropriated an inflatable pillow from the other cot and covered it with a clean towel.

She awakened later to the sound of a helicopter engine close by and shot an incredulous look at her watch as she struggled to her feet. Almost six o'clock—she'd slept away most of the afternoon!

She ran her fingers through her hair but didn't stop to comb it properly before going to the door of the tent house and peering around it at a silver helicopter hovering on the landing pad. She could see Wally's coveralled figure busily motioning for the pilot in the helicopter to punch off the steel cable which held a fuel barrel. Then the helicopter skids touched ground just long enough for a slight man wearing cotton pants and a down jacket to emerge. He ran to pick up the cable from the ground and shove it behind the pilot's seat. The door was secured while he moved out of danger beside Wally, keeping in a crouched position when under the still-turning rotors. The helicopter took off again after the two men gave a casual salute to the pilot, who responded with the traditional thumbs-up gesture.

It wasn't until Wally and the newcomer started back toward the tent houses that they noticed Carly standing by the doorway staring wonderingly after the fast-moving whirlybird.

"I decided that you were going to sleep the clock around," Wally said in his usual cheerful fashion as they came up to her. "Carly, this is Wing Loo, who cooks for us. Wing, this is Miss Carly Marshall— Nancy's sister."

The cook was a middle-aged Chinese whose ivory skin stretched without a wrinkle over his high cheekbones. His graying hair was cut so short that his head almost looked shaved. He beamed as he said, "Glad you could come, Miss Marshall. Has Wally found you enough to eat?"

"Plenty, thank you—and it was delicious." She ran a hand distractedly through her hair again as she said to the younger man, "I didn't mean to sleep so long."

"That's okay. We're in good shape now." Wally clapped Wing Loo on the back vigorously. "Our really important cargo arrived—that's what matters."

Carly's engaging smile included both of them. "It's a good thing, isn't it? My cooking talent's pretty limited."

" 'S okay. I'll take over now." Wing started for the cookhouse and then seemed to remember the newspaper he was carrying. "You want this?" he asked Wally. "I read it on the way."

The other reached for it with a lazy gesture, checking the headlines. "Anything new?"

Wing shrugged.

Wally continued to scan the front page. "They found some of those nuggets that were missing. Taxes are going up, and the cops say drug traffic's increasing in the state." He offered the newspaper to Carly. She took it as she shook her head admiringly at the Oriental cook. "I can't imagine being so relaxed in a helicopter that you could read the newspaper."

Wally burst out laughing. "She was flying Betsy with me every inch of the way."

Wing's thin gray eyebrows arched. "I don't blame her. When I fly with you, I do the same thing." He went into a spasm of laughter as he made his way to the mess hall.

"Everybody's a comic around here," Wally groused, and turned back to Carly. "How was your nap?"

"Fine, thanks." Her forehead creased as she surveyed the camp. "Are we still the only inhabitants?"

"That's right. And it'll stay that way—at least for tonight." He reached in his coverall pocket. "Want a stick of gum?"

"No, thank you." Carly hesitated, and then, when he didn't continue, she went on. "Did you talk to Patrick?"

"Yes, ma'am. Right on schedule." Wally was making a project out of unwrapping the gum. "He said he couldn't make it back to base tonight. Something probably came up."

"I see."

"Don't take it personally. Pat's a busy man," Wally said, trying to sound convincing. "He wanted to know if you were comfortable. I told him you were."

"Of course." She looked down at the newspaper, as if surprised to see it still in her hand. "Would Wing mind if I went in the kitchen and had some coffee?"

"Of course not. How about a can of beer?" Wally said, falling into step beside her.

She shook her head. "I need something to wake me up. That's the trouble with naps in the afternoon. I can't think what's wrong with me—I never take them when I'm at home. It must be the fresh air."

As she heard herself chattering on, it was like standing in the wings and listening to a performance. She was determined not to let on how Patrick's decision had affected her. There was a long, lonely night ahead and she'd have to play the part she'd been handed.

Even Stanislavski couldn't have found any fault with her performance for the rest of the evening. She chatted with the two men until dinner was ready and then managed enough of Wing's delicious chicken-tetrazzini casserole so that neither man suspected her loss of appetite.

When the dishes were done, she buried herself behind Wing's newspaper while he and Wally played gin rummy to a musical background provided by a battery cassette.

As soon as it was feasible, Carly folded the newspaper and tried to yawn convincingly. "I think I'll go to bed. Don't break up your game," she said when Wally and Wing both glanced up.

Wally shoved back his chair. "I was just going to take a look round and make sure there wasn't any wildlife in the compound. Never can tell." He paused to point a finger at Wing, who was adding the score. "Don't go away—I plan to get my money back."

Wing chuckled at the thought and gave Carly a shy good-night nod when she went past him to the door.

Wally caught up with her a few steps later. "What's the hurry? The night's still young. It won't even be dark until eleven." He reached out for the newspaper she had tucked absently under her arm.

"You've been wedded to this thing all night. What was so fascinating in it?"

"Nothing special." Since she had spent most of her time using it as a prop to hide behind and barely remembered what was on the front page, she was able to tell the truth for a change. The burst of honesty didn't last long though because she went on to say, "Wally, I think it would be better if I went back to Fairbanks tomorrow. Now that I've seen what a base camp looks like." She put out her palms in a graphic gesture. "There's not much for me to do. Besides, everybody's busy and I feel like an awful nuisance."

"That's a lot of rot! There isn't even anybody here for you to bother." He caught her arm and pulled up on the path, forcing her to do the same. "Wait a minute—you're not stewing about Pat's absence?"

"Of course not."

She must have sounded more convincing than she felt, because Wally nodded, and then he went on hesitantly. "Actually, Pat thought you might like to check out that cabin at the lake tomorrow. When there's any wildlife around, you'll see it there. If the plan sounds good, Wing can fix a lunch and I'll drop you off when I head for the fly camp tomorrow morning. We'll have to leave by seven-thirty," he warned. "Can you make it?"

"Can I!" Her tone throbbed with excitement before a remnant of caution made her ask, "You're sure that it's all right with Patrick?"

"Now, would I lead you astray on something so important?" He stuck his hands in his pockets and started on down the path with her. "You may have a pretty long day at the cabin before I can get back to pick you up. Will that bother you?"

"Of course not. Just so long as there's a tree to climb if the bears get thick."

They had reached her tent house, and Wally absently dug the toe of his boot in the hard-packed earth by the door. "Forget about trees. The cabin isn't in great shape, except for a nice thick door. If you see any bears, make damn sure you get behind it."

"Much more talk like that and I'll be afraid to step outside in the first place. What should I take with me?"

"Whatever art stuff you want. Wing'll put in sandwiches and coffee for your lunch, unless there's something you'd rather have."

"That sounds perfect!"

"Okay." He turned back toward the mess cabin, adding over his shoulder, "Don't worry about an alarm clock. I'll bang on your door on my way to the shower in the morning so you won't miss breakfast. G'night."

"G'night. And, Wally . . ."

His step slowed. "Yeah?"

"Thanks."

He merely grinned and went on his way.

Despite Carly's certainty that she wouldn't sleep a wink with such excitement in store, a deep, almost drugged sleep overtook her right after her head touched the pillow, and Wally's palm was needed on her door the next morning to bring her out of it.

She managed to shower and be at the mess hall just as Wing was opening the door to hammer an old piece of metal suspended outside.

Both he and Wally insisted that she tackle eggs and bacon for breakfast, when she would have settled for just juice and coffee.

"No way," Wally said, shoving a stack of buttered toast over in front of her before helping himself. "In this country, we eat as if every meal's our last one."

"That's a cheering thought." She stared at him. "Should I make out my will, too?"

"What he really means, Miss Marshall," Wing said

reprovingly as he approached with the coffeepot, "is that sometimes things go wrong with the flying schedules. The weather changes or the men are late for the pickup. I've put a few 'extras' in your lunch just in case things are delayed." He straightened after he'd finished pouring the coffee. "You like corned beef?"

"It's a favorite of mine," Carly said, biting into a piece of toast. "And I promise not to panic if the helicopter shuttle service is late. Patrick must keep you busy," she added to Wally.

"You can say that again." He looked at his watch and stood up, taking a last swallow of coffee as he lingered by the table. "I want to check out Betsy and make sure she's in good health. Finish your breakfast," he advised Carly. "You can have fifteen minutes or so while I'm doing it." He went over to take the food rucksack that Wing had left by the door, giving the cook a casual salute afterward. "See you tonight. I'll let you know if I'm picking up Hal."

The excitement didn't help Carly's appetite, but she managed to finish breakfast and get to the helicopter pad on time. She was wearing jeans and a plaid wool shirt topped with a poplin jacket, which seemed to meet with Wally's approval, but he raised an eyebrow at her canvas oxfords. "Those won't get you far," he said.

She hoisted her zipper carryall with her sketching materials behind the black vinyl seat of the helicopter. "Right now, they're the best I can do. Besides, I don't intend to get my feet wet." She fixed him with a stern glance. "Unless there are complications."

"Don't worry, Betsy's in good health and raring to go. Climb in and fasten your seat belt. Let's grab a patch of the wild blue." When she winced, he grinned, unabashed. "Pilots talk like that in television movies. I didn't want to disappoint you."

Five minutes later when they'd taken off and Betsy

was skimming forward, Wally raised his voice to say, "If you prefer a conventional announcement, I can furnish that too." He cleared his throat and droned, "This is Captain Burton speaking. Arctic Helicopter welcomes you to its Flight Number One for Fly Camp Able with our first stop at Discovery Lake. This morning we will be cruising mainly at five hundred feet on our north-bound journey. Our flight is approximately twenty-two minutes to touchdown and our estimated arrival time is eight-oh-two. At the right, you'll notice a fine view of the Alaska range. Below, you see the stunted forests that are found throughout this interior region. During the flight, you may see moose feeding, although we are too high to observe the low-brush species. In case of emergency, kindly remember the motto found on the mayonnaise jar in our lunch bag—'Keep cool but don't freeze.' We hope you enjoy your flight, and remember to book Arctic on your next journey."

Carly was giggling so hard that she forgot to be nervous. "You idiot! What on earth is a low-brush moose?"

"A rabbit, natch. Don't laugh. If Pat doesn't replenish Wing's larder in the next day or so, we may be having them for dinner."

"Do you fly in supplies from Fairbanks?"

He shook his head. "Not unless there's an emergency. Most everything's trucked to Ophir, and we pick it up there. This company's bank balance is healthy, but the hourly rate on a helicopter makes a banker turn gray. We only use them for the really important stuff."

Carly nodded absently and took a minute to admire the pale tendrils of clouds above them. The clear morning still bore the tang of autumn, but there was no disguising springtime's effect on the land below. The grasses under the dark spruce trees ranged from grayish-brown to pale green when viewed from the helicopter, and the isolated lakes mirrored all the grandeur in their pure unclouded waters. Carly drew a deep breath, wondering how she could be so lucky. Then, like all artists, wished passionately that she was talented enough to reproduce the scenic wonder in the way it deserved.

She was silent so long that Wally finally spoke up. "Are you still feeling okay?"

"Oh, fine, thanks." She half-turned to smile. "The view's so great that I've even forgotten to be nervous. If I stay up here much longer, you might have a convert on your hands."

"Better make up your mind this summer before the 'termination dust.' That's the name for our first snowfall. All the temporary workers in the field get their pink slips and head back to town. Once the weather changes in this part of the world, Mother Nature takes over with a vengeance." He added hastily, "Not that I want to change your mind. Lord knows, we could use some gorgeous new residents around here."

"You're doing all right the way things are. Laila looked pretty spectacular from what I saw."

"Spectacular and hard-to-get. Right now she's casting for something better from the pool." Before Carly could reply, Wally abruptly changed the subject. "There's where we're going! See that cabin on the lakeshore—just at the bottom of that small peak. You don't have to cross your fingers—those treetops aren't as close as they look."

Carly sincerely hoped that the granite sides of the mountain weren't either. She swallowed nervously as Wally directed the copter around the edge of the crag which jutted into the narrow part of the kidney-shaped lake. As Betsy lost altitude, Carly could see the hut on a narrow section of beach at the foot of the hill. The only place that looked possible for landing the helicopter was a grassy patch at one side of the cabin, and Wally headed for it. "Is this the fly camp?" she asked.

"Hell, no, that's on the other side of the hill. But don't try hiking over to go calling. Even the Dall sheep think twice before they use the trail. That's why not many people use this cabin; it's pretty inaccessible unless you fly in or like long-distance swimming in Discovery Lake." He gestured toward the expanse of water below. "This was all frozen until about two weeks ago. You can still see some pieces of ice at the shoreline. Hang on—this is a drafty place to land."

Carly kept her eyes on his sure hands rather than looking at the ground, which seemed to be rising exceptionally fast to meet them. Betsy was caught in a gust of wind, but Wally controlled the roll instantly, and within a minute the skids of the orange helicopter touched the ground almost simultaneously.

Carly was remembering that disastrous, lingering farewell he'd staged at the base camp the day before as she fumbled with the buckle on her seat belt. "You don't have to get out," she said. "I'll be okay."

Wally gave her a puzzled look but didn't cut the power to the rotors. "You'll need help carrying the lunch, won't you?"

"No, thanks, I can manage."

"Don't you want me to check the cabin for uninvited houseguests?"

That possibility made her hesitate. "Well, I'd appreciate it if you wait until I make sure that the coast is clear."

"Sure thing." He twisted in the seat and brought up the rucksack containing her lunch so she could handle it easily. As she opened the helicopter door, he caught her elbow warningly. "Keep your head down until you're clear of the rotors. Otherwise, you won't have to worry about bears or anything else. Understand?"

"I certainly do." She shuddered and said, "Lordy, what a way to go."

"I haven't yet heard of a good one."

"There's something in that, too." She clutched the rucksack to her breast as well as the carryall with her sketching materials and piled a thermos on top. "You *will* be back this afternoon?" She tried to sound casual, but the isolation of the hut suddenly loomed large in her thoughts. "I don't believe I'm the pioneering type."

He grinned at that. "I don't think you are, either. That's okay. You have some other fringe benefits."

"But about this afternoon . . ." she persisted.

"Don't worry, honey." Wally rubbed his swollen jaw with the back of his gloved hand. "Like Mafeking, you'll be relieved." Her amazed look made him grin. "During the long winter nights, we occasionally read books." He gestured toward the hut then. "Go take a look, and for God's sake keep your head down."

If Carly had drawn her head in any further, she would never have gotten it out of her collarbone later, but Wally gave her an approving thumbs-up gesture as she turned to look at him when she reached the old hunting cabin. She grinned back at him and then carefully pushed open the door.

After a swift glance around the barren interior, she let out a soft sigh of relief. The room was so sparsely furnished that anything bigger than a rabbit couldn't have been hiding there. Since Wally was waiting, she didn't linger but turned on the threshold and gave him an all-clear sign.

He nodded at her, and almost instantly Betsy's big rotors accelerated. The wild grasses on either side were flattened as the helicopter rose, and the powerful high-thrust engine noise was deafening in the solitude.

Carly turned her back to escape the resultant cloud of dust. When she twisted around a minute later, the orange whirlybird was at cruising altitude and half-way around the flank of the rugged peak. The throaty turbine sound had changed to a peculiar high-pitched buzzing noise, and as she watched, the helicopter went on to disappear from view.

A water bird on the lake behind her gave a piercing raucous call just then, and Carly turned so fast that the thermos she was carrying almost slithered to the ground. She gave a snort of self-derision when she saw the big white bird take off from the water with another mournful cry. She stared at it, fascinated, until a buzzing sound made her think for a minute that Wally was returning. Then she discovered a mosquito poised for attack on one knuckle while another hovered in a landing pattern in front of her nose.

She moved swiftly into the cabin and slammed the door behind her. While unloading her provisions on the rickety table which was pushed against one wall, she let her glance roam over the interior of the hut again. An instant later she heard a familiar whine around her head. "Damn!" she said fervently and hurried to place a piece of plastic screen over the small window cut into the chinked logs. Apparently it was the only protection against insects unless she put in the crude wooden shutter which was propped against the wall.

That would be an emergency measure, she decided, because it would also cut off the cabin's only daylight. A subdued whine disclosed that at least one mosquito was screened in, as effectively as his relatives were screened out. Carly hoped the odds were in her favor and poured some coffee from the thermos while she decided what to do with her day.

There was a pile of firewood for the potbellied stove which was used for heat and cooking. A metal film holder full of kitchen matches was on a crude shelf alongside two utilitarian white candles. That took care of the necessities, she thought, and let her gaze wander over the amenities. The cabin boasted a pair of wooden chairs which were short on padding and of garage-sale vintage, but she was glad to sit on one and drink her coffee.

If the chairs were of the bare-bones variety, the makeshift couch against the far wall was even worse. The wooden frame was barely six inches above the floor, with rawhide strips across it to make a mattress of sorts. Carly got up to inspect it more closely and found a monumental spider web at one end. She gave it a wide berth and walked over to stand in the sunshine which filtered through the screen at the window.

The small opening provided a condensed view of the lake, but Carly felt a sense of frustration engulf her. Surely she wasn't going to be kept inside just by a horde of mosquitoes.

She went back and rummaged through the rucksack to see what Wing had provided for lunch, discovering the wonderful man had put a tube of insect repellent, carefully wrapped in plastic, right on top. Not only mosquitoes had wings, she thought, helping herself lavishly to the salve. Angels had them, too—and Wing certainly deserved a pair for being so thoughtful! Now she could meet the aggressors and have a fighting chance.

When she emerged from the cabin a little later, she'd used the salve, donned a head scarf, and turned up her jacket collar as extra protection.

There were two empty oil drums discarded in the weeds next to the hut. She perched on the one which afforded a magnificent view of the lake and the narrow shoreline. Straight ahead was the snow-topped mountain range, providing a panorama just made to be sketched.

The rest of the day was pure enchantment. There were birds everywhere: land birds of every size whose nests were in the spruce and birch trees; and water birds with long legs and bills, on their migration from the south. The latter were feeding from the icy lake, and from the frenzied activity, Carly deduced there was no shortage of things on their menu. She remembered what she'd heard about the wonders of Alaskan fishing and decided it was one fish story that was true.

In the late afternoon she almost forgot to breathe when a pair of moose emerged at the lakeshore a hundred yards away. The marvelous animals browsed for fully fifteen minutes before disappearing into the trees at the bottom of the mountain behind the hut.

Just after they left, there was an unusual outcry from the birds on the other side of the cabin, and Carly caught sight of a burly straw-colored shape in the tall grass there.

She didn't wait to verify her suspicions; she scooped up her sketching materials in one fluid motion and dashed to the safety of the hut, closing the door and even dropping a wooden safety bar as a precaution.

Her pad and pencils were discarded on the table as she moved quickly across to the tiny screened window. The bear was out of sight at that angle, and she decided there was no need to close out her only source of light and fresh air with the wooden shutter.

She glanced automatically at her watch and gasped as she saw how late it was. Until then, she'd been so engrossed with her sketching that she hadn't noticed the time had fled. Now that she was reminded, hunger pangs confirmed it. Wing's picnic lunch had been eaten hours before.

As she stared out the window, she tried to remember if Wally had ever said what time he'd be returning, and finally had to admit defeat.

She knew there was no need to worry; there was a half-sandwich left, plus a banana and apple, so she wouldn't go hungry. Not even if she had to stay overnight. The stove and firewood would probably have the hut snug in no time, so heat wasn't a problem either.

A battered aluminum kettle on the shelf made her wish that she'd thought to get water earlier in the day. Certainly she'd have to bring some in before darkness fell.

She peered anxiously through the screen again, trying to see if the grizzly was still around. There was no way she'd risk running into him—even if it meant being holed up until morning.

For an instant she had visions of being incarcerated for weeks while the bear sat on the hut's front porch. Then she gave herself an angry shake. "Honestly!" she muttered in disgust, and absently started to peel the banana for something to do.

She'd just taken a bite when there was a grating noise nearby that made her almost choke on it. Her pulse rate shot up, sounding like a percussion solo in her ears, and she discovered that she had a death grip on the banana as she felt the mushy pulp in her palm. Like a robot, she stared at it foolishly for another thirty seconds, trying to decide what to do. Then common sense returned. She dropped the debilitated banana on the table, wiped her hand on her jeans, and hurried to shove the wooden shutter in place.

So it would be dark, she told herself—so what? Better dark and safe than staring nose-to-nose at a grizzly in the daylight.

Once the shutter was tight, she fumbled her way back to the candles on the shelf, calling herself all kinds of a fool for not lighting them before she shut out the daylight. There was another interval while she groped for the container of matches. Ten seconds later, she succeeded in knocking it to the floor. "Dammit to hell!" she snapped, forgetting all about bears in her anger. One thing was for sure, she wasn't going to crawl around on those grimy floorboards trying to find the matches.

Before she lost her nerve, she felt her way determinedly to the front door. It wouldn't hurt to open it just a sliver, she told herself. Just a crack—so light could come in and she could see where those miserable matches had rolled. After all, no self-respecting bear would approach a strange hut and scratch on the door. She was an utter fool for shutting herself in the darkness in the first place. After this, she'd light the candles and wait ten minutes before she looked outside again.

Her logic made so much sense that she was almost humming with satisfaction when she finally discovered the crude wooden bar on the door. She lifted it and started to pull the heavy old door open, when she heard movement outside.

She froze, but the door catapulted open. As she stumbled aside, a huge creature loomed in front of her, and she let out a terrified scream that must have been heard in Prudhoe Bay. She screamed again as she felt a weight on her shoulder.

Mercifully, then, darkness descended even as her knees buckled and the floor rose to meet her.

6

<hr/>

The gray oblivion didn't last very long. Carly was sure of that, because she was being lowered onto that dusty thong mattress when her eyelids fluttered open again. She started to struggle upward until she realized her head was against a padded down jacket instead of a fur coat. "After I get my breath back," she murmured, "I think I'll kill you."

"You took twenty years off my life with that first scream," Patrick ground out as he straightened and stared down at her. "Lie still, dammit, or you'll pass out again."

"I would have been better off to let the bear come in," she said somewhat bitterly, pushing up on her elbow. It was hard to maintain the position, because there were more holes in the mattress than there were thongs. After two tries she levered herself into a sitting position against the wall.

"I told you to lie down." Patrick looked up from

his search through her rucksack. "Isn't there any food around here?"

She shook her head. "Just bears. In their natural organic state. Would you please close that door?"

Patrick's black brows came together. "What for?"

"Because there's a grizzly walking around out there. Or he was—five minutes ago. I'm surprised you didn't notice him when you came off the path on the mountain." She saw him stare incredulously at her across the room. "Please—would you humor me just this once?"

Patrick rubbed the back of his neck and then apparently decided to go along with her wishes. "Okay—just wait until I light this candle."

A flare of annoyance made her stir restlessly. He *would* know the right way to go about things. If she'd been equally sensible, she wouldn't be where she was now. Although when she thought about it, the rough bed frame wasn't all that bad. Not after perching on an unyielding oil drum for most of the day. She ignored the possibility that her uplifted spirits might have something to do with the presence of the tall man who was intent on getting a candle to stand upright in a chipped saucer. When he succeeded, he put the candle on the table and then walked over to close the door. "I think your furry friend is miles away by now, but we can hole up for a little while." He paused in the middle of the room. "Are you feeling better?"

For Patrick, the tone was amazingly gentle and concerned. It took Carly by such surprise that it was an instant or two before she could reply. "Yes, thanks. I'm sorry to have been so stupid. My imagination was working overtime, and it was so dark in here that the daylight blinded me. All I saw was a tall figure—that's why I screamed," she finished apologetically.

A slow grin creased his face. "It was sure as hell effective. I almost turned tail and ran."

"I'll bet." She fingered a button on her jacket self-consciously. "Anyhow, I'm glad that it's over."

"Don't start giving thanks too soon. There's some news you haven't heard yet."

"Nothing's happened to Wally?" Alarm made her voice strained. "He didn't have an accident?"

"Not in the way you mean," Patrick replied. "He just isn't happy about something in Betsy's innards, and it's going to take until morning to check it out. That's why I'm here—bearing the glad tidings."

"I thought it must be something like that. Otherwise, you certainly wouldn't have attempted the trail over the mountain from your fly camp. Wally told me how difficult it is." She frowned as a thought suddenly occurred to her. "Does that mean that we have to go back tonight?"

"It'll be dark in an hour or so."

Carly wondered what his evasive answer meant. Did he plan to go back alone, or was he asking if she could make it, even if they had to wait out the hours of darkness at the side of the trail? "With maybe a bear for company," she said, thinking aloud.

"I beg your pardon?"

She stared at him suspiciously. "It probably seems ridiculous to you, but if you don't mind, I'd really rather wait here. I'd be terrified to be stuck overnight on a mountain trail in this part of the world."

"You're sure?" His gesture encompassed the Spartan furnishings of the hut. "It won't be easy."

She swallowed as she considered and then smiled. "I'll manage." When he continued to stare at her, she added, "You'll want to be going. I'm sorry that there isn't some coffee left from lunch—you could probably use it before you tackle that climb again."

He rubbed the side of his nose reflectively and

seemed to reach a decision. "If you're staying here, I'll stay, too. It's probably the sensible thing," he went on before she could reply. "I'll get back to the fly camp in the morning and radio for Wally to pick you up here. Now I'd better go get my rucksack—there's some food in it, which should help our cause. You stay in here," he added when she started to get to her feet. "Just in case that grizzly of yours is still around."

"But what about you?"

"I've got a pistol with the rest of my stuff. That's standard equipment for geologists working in the field up here," he went on in a matter-of-fact tone. "So far, I've never had to use it."

"You *will* be careful?" She realized how foolish she sounded even as the words came out, and was glad of the shadows in the room so that he couldn't see the blush which warmed her cheeks.

"Very careful." He paused with his hand on the door. "Make sure you keep this closed. We can open it later, once I know the coast is clear."

He was gone without waiting for her answer. Carly saw the door close firmly behind him, and when he didn't immediately reappear, she heaved a sigh of relief. Evidently the grizzly had gone on his way, too.

She cupped her palms over her flushed cheeks, vowing that she'd conduct herself properly in the future. The next few hours were going to be difficult enough without behaving like a headstrong ingenue.

She frowned as she gingerly tested the heated skin on her cheekbones, realizing she'd collected a sunburn during the hours she'd spent outside. Her frown deepened when she encountered a mosquito bite, as well. More than one, she found, and discovered it required all her willpower to avoid scratching the vulnerable spots. In desperation she went to light the other candle. Anything to take her mind off the subject.

Patrick found her sitting in a wooden chair with her hands determinedly clasped in her lap when he came back a little later. He was carrying an orange nylon rucksack in one hand and a holstered .44 Magnum pistol in the other. The rucksack was dumped on the table, but he handled the gun with considerably more care as he put it on the wooden shelf. "The coast's clear for bigger wildlife," he announced. "Unfortunately, there's no shortage of bugs. We can take the shutter off the window, but we'll be more comfortable keeping the door closed. Once we start a fire, the smoke will thin our mosquito population."

She nodded agreement and stood up to remove the shutter, glad of something to do. Afterward, she watched him go down on one knee to start a blaze in the potbellied stove. "I hope it works. I've just discovered that my insect repellent wasn't totally successful."

He grinned at her careful choice of words. "I know what you mean. We had a camp last summer where the horseflies were so big that if you killed one, you needed a friend to help carry it out of the tent. Wally saw a whopper land at base camp and claimed he almost went out and put gas in him."

Carly giggled, enchanted with this new side of Patrick. Of course, he was simply trying to divert her, but it was marvelous anyhow.

"In Fairbanks, the top-selling record is a ditty called 'Sounds of Summer.' Features a mosquito chorus and flies rubbing their wings together." He grinned across at her after lighting the fire. "There's another pesky rhythm group Alaska has called White Sox. Their bite's like a mule kick."

"*Now* you tell me."

He nodded commiseratingly. "A head net is the

best thing for protection. You wear it with a brimmed hat."

She started to giggle again. "That could make some things difficult."

He didn't pretend to misunderstand. "Damned difficult. If anybody wanted to get romantic, they'd have to bring along a head net built for two."

"That would take away some of the enchantment," she said solemnly.

Patrick snorted. "To put it mildly." He walked over and picked up the battered kettle. "Might as well get some water for coffee."

"I can do that." Carly decided to show she wasn't a total loss. Then she had to spoil it by asking, "Do I get it from the lake?"

Pat opened his mouth and closed it again, nodding instead.

Obviously he had decided to turn over a new leaf in being agreeable, Carly decided, and followed him to the door. "You don't have to come with me," she said hastily.

"I wasn't going to." His gaze swept the grassy plain that constituted the hut's front yard after he opened the door. "All clear. Don't fall in." He shoved the kettle in her hands and turned back into the hut.

Carly directed a withering glance toward his shoulder blades and then grinned as she recognized the futility of her gesture. She strolled down to the lakeside, delighted to be out in the fresh air again. The western sky was ablaze with the sunset's fire, and she stood savoring it for a moment, until she knelt and filled the kettle with water.

She turned her attention then to the Arctic lake whose edges made a vibrant blue binding against the muted earth tones of the shore. The icy depths of the water looked forbiddingly deep. When she'd viewed the lake from a helicopter, it was an even gray-blue expanse with none of the appealing color gradation found in warmer areas.

Her eyes narrowed as she watched a tern swoop over the surface, glad that he was the only one getting his feet wet. Or almost the only one, she amended, as water splashed from the kettle when she started back to the hut. "Damn and blast!" she said, trying to brush the lingering drops from her pants leg.

Her antics startled a plump squirrel that was going past with a dirt-encrusted peanut in his mouth. He darted for the corner of the cabin and whisked up to the ridgepole, safely beyond reach. Then he relaxed and started efficiently shelling the peanut.

Carly grinned at his preoccupied stance and said, "I'd like to know where you found that. We could share the wealth," before going inside.

"Who were you talking to?" Patrick said idly, watching her use both hands to steady the kettle onto the stove top.

"A bushy-tailed permanent resident." She dried her fingers on a handkerchief from her jacket pocket. "You don't grow peanuts in Alaska, do you?"

"Not that I've heard of."

"Then that squirrel knows something we don't. He was shelling one for his dinner." She moved over to look at the meager leftovers from her lunch spread on the table. "He's better off than we are."

"I won't argue with that. Some of the fellows were probably feeding him when they stopped by last week." Seeing her puzzled look, Patrick added, "We use this as a fishing camp when we have some spare time." He paused. "Too bad we can't fall back on the standard staple in this part of the country for our dinner tonight."

"What's that?"

"Golden soup. Named in honor of the gold rush, of course." His tone was bland.

"Golden soup." She frowned and tried to remember. "I've never heard of it. How do you make it?"

"First off, you boil fourteen karats . . ." He stopped at her agonized groan. "Sorry—you did ask."

"Any more jokes like that and I'll go talk to my squirrel."

"Wait a minute!" Patrick snapped his fingers, making her start with surprise. "I think I left some fishing line cached in a burned stump last season. I'll go see. With any luck, we can have fish for dinner."

"May I come and watch?" She was at his heels as he headed for the door. "I promise I won't make any noise."

"Better not." He paused on the threshold. "The stovepipe is almost rusted through at the cabin roof. We have a rule that somebody has to stick around and keep an eye on the fire."

"Oh." Her subdued response showed her disappointment. "Well, at least I can watch you through the window."

He shook his head. "The best fishing place is around the bend—out of sight. Just keep your fingers crossed and make sure the water doesn't burn."

With a quick wink he was gone. Carly turned to check the water on the stove before his words penetrated, and then she shoved her hands in her pockets and stalked over to the window, determined to watch as long as there was anything to see.

It only took a minute or two before Patrick's lean figure disappeared into the nearest grove of stunted trees. Carly chewed on her lip in frustration, wishing that he'd stop wrapping her in cotton just because she'd blacked out for a while.

She turned back to survey the stovepipe, failing to see any evidence of its rusted parts. For an instant she was tempted to ignore Patrick's orders and follow him. Then she recognized the folly of such behavior and went back to sit on a chair by the table.

A little later she hunched it closer to the stove. The sun might not be completely down, but its warmth had disappeared and the air felt more like January than May. She remembered that she could have been partway up the mountain trail, and decided to start appreciating the hut's amenities.

Not that they didn't afford complications. Her thoughtful gaze went to the austere cot in the corner. Aside from its lack of padding, it was barely wide enough for one person, let alone two. Of course, there was a chance that Patrick would stretch out on the wooden floor.

At that point, her common sense rebelled. No man in his right mind would choose to lie on that rough, dusty wooden floor if there was any other possibility.

But what about the great outdoors? Maybe he liked fresh air.

As she thought about it, she was absently scratching a good-sized mosquito bite which had materialized on her thumb. She frowned down at it and then decided it was better to concentrate on that rather than more difficult subjects.

It was the only sensible thing to do. For one thing, she had run out of excuses. For another, she knew that Patrick would make up his own mind, and, in the process, probably make up hers, as well.

Not that she would automatically go along with it unless she chose to. The last decision came after she realized that sharing a cot with the man might not be too unpleasant. All things considered.

That thought brought a sudden surge of heat to her body, and she walked restlessly over to the window. Surprising how much warmth a potbellied stove could generate, she told herself, knowing very well that the water in the kettle was barely tepid.

It had just reached the boiling point when she heard Patrick's welcome steps on the gravel in front of the hut. She rushed to meet him at the door, feeling as if he'd been gone for months instead of minutes.

He was dangling two cleaned lake trout on a thin peeled branch from one hand and carried what appeared to be a nylon tarp under his other arm. "I hope you like trout for dinner," he said briskly, tossing the tarp onto the cot as he walked in. "Our menu's a little limited tonight. If you're allergic to fish, it's practically nonexistent."

"You can't get rid of me that way," she said, admiring his catch. "Do we have to wait and bake these in the coals, or can you do sleight of hand and make a frying pan appear?"

"Have they ditched that frying pan again?" His annoyed glance raked the shelf behind her. "Hold the fort—I'll be right back." He went out the door and was back thirty seconds later carrying a smoke-blackened frying pan.

Carly stared at him. "Do you do rope tricks in your spare time?" she asked finally.

"Nothing magical about it. We've found that it's better to stash the frying pan in that washtub hanging outside by the door. Otherwise, cooking utensils have a tendency to disappear." He was searching through his rucksack as he spoke, and gave a pleased exclamation as he pulled out a can. "I *thought* I had that along. Bacon," he explained, taking a knife from his pocket and finding the can-opener blade. "So our trout won't stick to the pan."

"I *know* what the bacon's for," Carly said. Her eyes narrowed as she surveyed his rucksack suspiciously. "Are you sure that you don't have caviar in there, or truffles hidden behind the ridgepole?"

"Sorry, just tea and instant coffee."

"What about that stump where you hid the fish-line? Is that where the tarp came from?"

Patrick nodded as he put strips of bacon in the frying pan atop the stove. "It's a remnant of another fishing trip when we were caught in the rain. I'm just sorry that it isn't a down comforter. The temperature drops in the middle of the night, and that jacket of yours doesn't look very warm. Didn't Wally tell you what kind of clothes to bring?"

Carly visibly relaxed at his familiar biting tones. "A weekend with the grizzlies wasn't on my original itinerary," she countered. "And down jackets don't fit into my budget right now. Besides, poplin is warmer than it looks. I'll be fine," she added, hoping that she sounded convincing.

"We'll see," he replied noncommittally, shaking the frying pan and turning the bacon with a fork.

"I can do that," Carly said, going over to stand at his elbow. "I wish you'd let me help."

"You can set the table and then make us some coffee. I think there's enough cutlery and dishes to see us through. Bring one of those plates over here, will you? This bacon's ready."

His casual acceptance of her presence implied an intimacy which set Carly's cheeks flaming again. She turned hurriedly to do his bidding, knowing that her attempt to keep things equally casual was failing dismally.

It didn't get any better. She dropped the spoon she used to measure instant coffee and almost sent a candle flying when she brushed it with her arm. Desperately she tried for a topic to cloak her disasters. "Wally mentioned Toklat was at a fly camp. You didn't leave him alone when you came to rescue me, did you?"

Patrick looked up from the frying pan, not bothering to hide his amusement. "Tok's a big dog now.

Don't you think he could manage one night on his own?"

"Of course, but . . ." She broke off and bent to straighten a fork on the table rather than hold his glance. "You know what I mean. I thought he'd be lonesome."

Patrick snorted. "As long as there's a roof over his head and food in his dish, Tok doesn't lose any sleep. Besides, he's with Hal tonight, so you won't have to lose any sleep either. On that score."

Carly shot him a startled look, but Patrick was slipping the trout into the frying pan and intent on his task. She bit her lip, aware that she was searching for a hidden meaning in every sentence he uttered. There was no reason to assume he'd make a pass merely because they were in such an isolated place. He'd announced that he found her desirable in Fairbanks, and later set a new speed record for going to bed—alone. Not that she would have allowed anything else, she told herself hastily, and jumped a good two inches when Patrick spoke again. "I beg your pardon?" she said, knocking the salt shaker over in the bargain.

"Nothing important." He frowned slightly as he saw her hastily right the salt. "I just said that Wing would do these faster and better. Are you sure you're okay? Not feeling faint again?"

"No—of course not." Carly shoved her hands in her jeans pockets and moved a safe distance from the table. "It looks to me as if you're doing fine in the food department. How could Wing do any better?"

"He has some special breading for fish. Mixes it himself."

"Then it must be good. Everything he fixed for dinner last night was delicious. He's nice, too." Carly walked over to the screen and peered through the twilight toward the quiet lake. "You must be pretty talented as well. Otherwise you couldn't have caught those trout and cleaned them in such a short time. It's a wonder that every fisherman in the lower forty-eight isn't up here trying his luck."

There was a clatter as the fork Patrick was using to turn the trout slipped from his grasp and dropped onto the stove top. "Damn!" he said as he retrieved it and succeeded in searing his fingertips in the process.

"Are you all right?" she asked worriedly as he muttered something unprintable under his breath.

"Of course." His tone was almost brusque. "Bring those plates over, will you? This is ready to eat."

Carly carried the plates one at a time so she'd be sure of getting their dinner safely back to the table. She watched him shove the empty frying pan to the back of the stove and tip some water in for soaking before he came and pulled out the chair opposite her. "I forgot to ask about your arm after that fracas the other night," she said as they picked up their forks. "I hope it isn't bothering you."

"It was just a scratch." Patrick reached for his coffee cup and took a swallow. "I gather that you didn't have any unwelcome visitors the next day."

"That's right." She eyed him curiously. "Was that an educated guess?"

"Partly. I checked with the police in the morning before I left. They promised to keep watch on the house for the next night or so."

She heaved a mock sigh. "So much for feminine intuition."

"What does that mean?"

"Just that I thought you might be suffering from an attack of conscience about leaving me alone in the house. So much that you changed your mind and invited me out to camp."

He concentrated on removing a bone from the succulent trout. "Sorry, now you'll have to guess again."

His noncommittal reply made her more daring. "I don't think you'd tell me if I had the right answer."

He looked up then and met her gaze squarely. "Why not? I admitted once before that I found you desirable. I haven't changed my mind."

His calm declaration almost made Carly choke on a swallow of coffee. She used both hands to lower the cup to the table so that she wouldn't spill it, as well. "That's ridiculous—you know it is."

"In what way?" He sounded almost clinical.

"Well, you weren't charmed to see me when I arrived. For a minute, I even thought you were going to send me back to Ophir."

"I couldn't. There wasn't room in the copter."

She ignored his attempt to gloss it over. "You know what I mean."

"I do indeed." He looked at her thoughtfully. "And I owe you an apology. My only excuse is that I hate to be kept waiting, and everything possible had gone wrong."

"But I didn't keep Wally waiting . . ." she began, and then subsided. There was nothing to be gained by going over it again. Far better to keep things as they were, considering the long night ahead. She cast a covert glance across the table, but it was hard to judge anything from Patrick's impassive expression. He was eating with every evidence of enjoyment, and Carly found herself wishing that she could equal his lack of concern. She was too acutely conscious of his broad-shouldered figure, more formidable than ever with the sleeveless down vest which he wore over a long-sleeved plaid shirt. He looked tough and assured, able to cope with anything.

"More coffee?"

She heard his question and blinked, coming back to reality in a hurry. It took an instant longer before she could check the contents of her own cup. "No, thanks. I still have some."

"You're not making much of an inroad on that trout," he commented, returning to the table after adding hot water to his own cup from the kettle still simmering on the stove.

"It's very nice, but I guess I'm too excited to eat." Then, so he wouldn't get the wrong idea, she added hurriedly, "You may take helicopters and grizzly bears for granted, but they have a strange effect on my digestion."

Patrick didn't pursue the subject. He nodded and put his cup on the table, picking up his empty plate. "Don't worry about it. If you're finished, I'll take care of the dishes and the remains."

Carly was relieved for any break in the tension which had been building. She helped scrape their dishes and followed Patrick when he carried the kettle of heated water outside.

He deposited it on the upended oil drum where Carly had perched for most of the afternoon and said, "I'm an old hand at this. There's no need for you to hang around. Don't wander too far, though—there's not much daylight left."

Carly nodded, grateful for his casual directive, and turned to disappear around the corner of the hut when he bent to his dishwashing.

He was back in the cabin when she returned, standing by the table and finishing his coffee. "I'll wash this in the lake tomorrow," he said when the cup was empty. "The Board of Health would never sanction our operation, but we all survive." He jerked his head toward the stove top, where the kettle had been refilled with water. "That should get a little warm before the fire dies down, if you want some."

"I'm okay, thanks."

He took a closer look then and noted that her complexion was damp and glowing. "That lake water's better for waking you up than putting you to sleep."

"Is that a threat or a promise?" she asked lightly.

"We'll wait and see."

As he went over to close the door, she noticed that he'd put the shutter in the window and rearranged the two candles on the table before she returned. The slamming of the door made her realize again how isolated they were, and she was glad that the flickering candlelight didn't mirror her nervousness. If Patrick had any inkling, he'd be thoroughly enjoying the situation. She saw him start to unbutton his padded vest, and her eyes widened incredulously. "You're . . . you're not going to take off your clothes?"

Even in that shadowed interior, it was impossible to miss his reaction to her gauche question, but he managed to keep his voice creditably solemn. "Not many of them." He was shrugging out of the vest as he spoke. "This is for you. Wear it on top of that jacket and it will keep out some of the drafts. We can wrap the tarp around us when we lie down. It's too bad that there isn't enough wood to keep the fire going all night. I didn't think we'd need it . . ." He stopped in mid-sentence and then finished lamely, "Probably should have stuck a hatchet in my pack."

"I think you were wonderful to even get here." Carly managed not to retreat as he moved close in front of her and helped her on with the vest. He solemnly directed her arms through the proper holes and then bent over to button the front, once she had it on.

Carly stared at the top of his head like one mesmerized. Evidently she wasn't the only one who'd utilized the lake, because his sleek dark hair gleamed with moisture in the candlelight. As his fingers moved up to another button, she hoped that he couldn't hear the way her heart was thundering in her breast.

Something must have given her away, because suddenly she felt his strong fingers fumble and then they ripped the vest open in one decisive gesture. "The hell with it!" he groaned, even as he caught the back of her hair with one hand and yanked her tight against him with the other.

Before she could manage a word, his mouth came down to cover hers.

There was no chance to do anything other than submit to that possessive embrace. His tongue probed gently at first, seeking purposefully before his lips hardened. Even if she'd had the inclination to resist, Patrick's expertise would have probably won her over. His hands moved surely, arousing feelings that she'd only suspected she possessed.

A moment—or was it aeons?—later, he raised his head and brushed his lips insistently across the soft hollow below her ear. "Let's go over and try to get comfortable," he murmured, as he moved her toward the cot. "This is a hell of a place to make love. Your sense of timing is terrible, my love. It's a good thing that you've other assets to make up for it." He pulled her down onto the thong mattress beside him and slid the vest from her shoulders. "I can keep you warm without this extra upholstery." His arm went around her again when the vest was discarded on the mattress.

As Patrick laced his fingers in her hair, obviously enjoying its silky texture, his glance met her flustered one. "Darling, don't look so surprised," he said lazily. "We only needed this to sort out our differences. It's a pity we didn't try it earlier."

She reached up to trace the line of his jaw with a slender finger. "I seem to remember a comment of yours in Fairbanks about meeting me later in New York. *If* it fit into your schedule."

"You needn't remind me." His voice was muffled because he was placing a kiss at the V neckline of her shirt. "It certainly wasn't one of my smarter ideas, but I wasn't sure how you felt then. Besides, you were Nancy's sister. Hardly fair game."

Carly stirred uneasily as she heard that. She didn't move far away, just enough to look up and check his expression. "What changed your mind?"

"Darling, you don't have to keep on that tack any longer. Thank the Lord, you were mature enough to know what you wanted. Otherwise, we'd probably still be sniping at each other out of sheer frustration. As it is, I figure you cost me three nights' sleep because you're such a distracting wench."

His deep tone made Carly's defenses crumble, and she almost capitulated then and there. Only feminine curiosity made her hold him off long enough so she could say, "I still don't understand. What do you mean—about knowing what I wanted?"

It was clear that Patrick wasn't in the mood for talk, and it showed when he sighed impatiently and leaned his head against the wall. "When you came on up here to the hut. I admit that I was madder than hell when I first heard, but then I had to admire your nerve. Only a woman who knew what she wanted would be that honest with a man. What the devil!" His last exclamation came when Carly yanked out of his arms, putting a considerable distance between them on the cot. "Dammit, now what's the matter?" he wanted to know.

She glowered at him, clutching her arms over her breast as the cold air made itself felt when she was deprived of his warm embrace. "If that isn't like a man!" She almost spat the words out. "Taking it for granted that I'd become a sex-starved camp follower—just to satisfy your monumental ego! I'm glad that I found out in time."

Patrick's eyes narrowed dangerously as he straightened. "You sound like Little Nell strapped to the railroad track. I didn't notice you suffering a few minutes ago." Her involuntary shiver made him growl, "For God's sake, put on that vest or you really will have something to complain about."

Carly started to protest and then reached for it reluctantly. She had no doubt that he'd put it on her if she didn't agree, and just then, it was safer to keep at arm's length.

Patrick watched her fumble with the buttons as he added sardonically, "Then I gather you didn't insist on coming here to spend the night with me?"

She found it was difficult to draw herself up haughtily on a rawhide cot that was almost resting on the floor. She managed to get her knees at a more dignified angle and turned to face him. "Wally told me that *you'd* issued the invitation."

"You're sure that you didn't misunderstand him?"

His irony made her cheeks get hot. "Hardly. I was all ready to go back to Fairbanks after the way you treated me at base camp. I presume you *did* ask me there," she said, mocking him. "Or did you think I was throwing myself at you even then?"

"There's no need to chew the scenery," Patrick said coldly. "I invited you to base camp. I *didn't* invite you up here. Either it was an honest misunderstanding or Wally decided he'd stir things up."

"I can't imagine why." Carly had regained her composure, but it was impossible to ignore the despairing numbness that was spreading through her.

Patrick continued relentlessly. "Then tell me why he radioed that you were here at the cabin and expecting company."

"Probably because he couldn't get back to pick me up—the way he promised. I would have been perfectly all right by myself overnight. There was no need for you to be inconvenienced," she continued, implying it was especially difficult for a man of his age and stamina.

Patrick reacted with the same lack of tact. "Don't worry, I'll survive. I'm not sure whether you would have—considering the way I found you."

"Well, now that I've recovered, you can leave anytime," she sputtered. "The sooner the better."

"It's too damned bad that you'll have to put up with me until daylight." Patrick heaved himself erect and tossed the tarp in her lap with a forceful gesture. "Take that and wrap yourself up in it nice and tight. Along with all those inhibitions you've cherished so long. And don't worry about having to share that cot—your reputation may be a little tarnished after tonight, but everything else will be still intact."

"Go to hell!" With one fluid motion she threw off the tarp and lunged to her feet. Her open hand had almost reached his cheek when he caught her wrist in a grip that hurt.

"Don't try that again or you'll really regret it." He glared down at her, annoyed to find that she had never looked lovelier than at that moment. Her silky hair was tousled, her brown eyes sparking with anger. His own eyelids narrowed to mask his thoughts, but his hand went up, unbidden, to smooth a thick strand of her hair from her face.

She gulped and took a deep breath to steady herself in his iron clasp. "Don't!" she protested. "Don't touch me. . . ."

He paid no attention. Deliberately his grasp on her hair tightened and he pulled her against him. "I'll do what I damn well please," he told her in a rough, uneven tone.

There wasn't time for him to say any more, because his mouth came down to cover hers—only this time there was no gentleness or compassion, only desire and passionate need.

Seconds later, he groaned and pushed her away from him. Carly had to clutch the edge of the table to keep her balance. Dimly she heard the cabin door open and close. When she finally managed to focus in the shadowed room, it was too late. Patrick had gone.

7

---◦━◦▬◈▬◦━◦---

Anger and chagrin vied with Carly's wounded pride during the rest of that long night.

For the first hour she managed to remain upright on one of the unyielding wooden chairs. She only had to recall some of Patrick's choicer remarks and her back would straighten defensively. During the rest of the time, she compiled a mental list of the scathing things she had forgotten to mention.

As time passed, her hopes diminished in that regard. It was bad enough to come out second best in the altercation, downright humiliating when Patrick took himself out of range. If that was the kind of man he was, far better that she should discover it now.

She got up and went over to open the door a crack—merely for fresh air, she told herself. The fresh air came in—accompanied by insects aplenty. Carly ducked as a mosquito dive-bombed, and shut the door so hard that it vibrated on the hinges.

She picked up the tarp that Patrick had left behind and wrapped it around herself before huddling on the rawhide cot. The down vest that he'd ordered her to wear was toasty warm, and she found herself wishing she'd had sense enough to bring a pair of down pants, as well.

It would have been more honorable if she'd insisted that he take the vest back. A woman wasn't entitled to pick and choose. According to history, she was supposed to take what the gods offered. The remembrance of what one god had offered made Carly groan and close her eyes, wishing that he hadn't been so convincing with his wares. That depressing thought was foremost in her mind when she finally fell into a troubled sleep.

It was the raucous call of the water birds which finally awakened her the next morning. She sat up, feeling thoroughly chilled in the early-morning air, and fumbled to get free of the enveloping tarp.

The fire had died down in the stove and the candles were guttered nubs. Carly stared around the room and rubbed a weary hand over her face. She felt as if she'd only been asleep for an hour or two and could scarcely believe it when she went over to open the door and check her watch in the daylight. Six o'clock. No wonder the birds were making a racket!

She yawned as she stood in front of the cabin, trying to appear casual as her glance covered the shoreline. As she suspected, there wasn't a trace of Patrick Donovan. She trudged down to the lake's edge and splashed some chilled water on her face as she tried to think what she should do next.

At any other time, she would've been entranced by the pale sunlight on the still-snowy peaks in the Alaska range. The stark gray-and-white contrast of the shadowed mountainsides would've been startling on its own, even without the additional brilliance of the green foliage on the lower slopes. When combined with the gray-blue of the quiet lake, the panorama was breathtaking. Small wonder that the cranes and wild geese were noisy with enthusiasm.

A sudden movement in the tangled grass nearby made Carly freeze as she started to walk back to the cabin. Then she identified a rabbit that was equally reluctant at making her acquaintance. She watched it disappear around the corner of the cabin and frowned as she noted a small pile of firewood stacked against the hut. It hadn't been there the day before—she was sure of it. Patrick must have collected it earlier to keep the fire going through the night.

The chilly breeze which lifted her hair made her decide to use the unexpected largess. Life would be more attractive if she could heat water for coffee.

It wasn't difficult to get the fire going, because she found a starter in the rucksack that Patrick had left behind when she rummaged for matches. There was also some canned bacon left, and a clean frying pan to cook it.

Even in his absence, Patrick was responsible for her well-being.

No doubt he was halfway over the mountain trail by then, en route to his fly camp. There was also no doubt in Carly's mind that he would arrange for someone to pick her up as soon as it could be arranged. With two helicopters at his command, he wouldn't waste any time in sending her on her way.

He was enough of a gentleman that he wouldn't come right out and ask her to leave base camp. On the other hand, Carly was equally sure that he wouldn't reappear while she was there.

Which left her one thing to do: get back to Fairbanks as soon as possible. After that, she'd leave a note for Nancy and take the next plane going south . . . or west . . . or east. Anywhere beyond Patrick Donovan's boundaries.

There was nothing like the cold morning light for looking at things in an honest perspective. Her anger of the night before had been replaced by a desolate empty feeling—a numbness that wouldn't go away.

She grimaced ruefully as she waited for the water to boil. Not even a cup of coffee could do anything to assuage that.

She should have been forewarned after their first meeting at the airport. Sparks only flew when there was a conflagration between a man and a woman. She'd spent a lifetime reading about such encounters and then failed to recognize the danger signs when they occurred.

Patrick had been honest enough to warn her of the perils that first night in Fairbanks. When she'd arrived in base camp, he'd kept her at arm's length and used Laila Anson as a safety buffer.

Now, thanks to a colossal misunderstanding, there was no hope of salvaging anything for the future. Patrick wasn't the type of man to take no for an answer. Last night, he hadn't even been interested enough to stay and make Carly change her mind.

She shoved her hands in her pockets and walked over to open the door, staring through it bleakly. If only Wally hadn't engineered the misunderstanding in the first place.

She had decided that she'd never know the reason why, when the angry buzzing sound that had become so familiar could be heard in the distance. Her pulse accelerated as Betsy's bulbous orange shape came around the south side of the peak, retracing the approach route.

Carly started toward the cleared area where the helicopter had landed before, and then stopped. If Patrick were aboard, she couldn't go blithely out and greet him as if nothing had happened. Not in front of Wally's keen eyes.

After touchdown, the helicopter's rotors barely stopped turning before Wally bounded down. "Hullo, hullo, hullo," he greeted her. "How does it feel to be listed as first priority?"

"I don't know what you're talking about." Carly slipped out from under the casual arm he draped across her shoulders as they turned back toward the hut. "I won't keep you waiting, though. It will just be a second while I gather up my stuff."

"Take your time. At least, up to five minutes or so." Wally beamed down as he walked beside her. He was in his customary coveralls, but his visored cap was squarely atop his head for a change. If he'd lost any sleep achieving Betsy's repairs, it wasn't evident in his clear-eyed gaze, and even the bruise on his jaw had subsided to a conventional hue. "Since you rate in the VIP category, the boss has put some elastic in my schedule," he went on.

Carly pulled up just inside the cabin door. "You've seen him this morning?" She tried to keep her tone uncaring, but there was no disguising the anxiety on her face. "There wasn't any problem getting to the fly camp?"

"Guess not. Why should there be?" Wally shrugged. "I didn't see him, but he was on the radio to base camp this morning. Routed Wing out of bed at an ungodly hour and left orders that I was to come and get you pronto. If Betsy wasn't flying, he'd bring in the other copter."

"I see." Carly kept her face averted as she picked up her belongings and shrugged the rucksack onto her shoulder. "I think that's everything."

Wally picked up the other rucksack. "This looks like Pat's. We'd better take it along."

"The tarp belongs to him, too." Carly had folded it neatly and put it on the cot. "Does that go?"

"I guess so. It's not like Pat to leave stuff scattered behind him." Wally gave her a droll sidelong glance. "He must have had other things on his mind."

"I'll go ahead and get in Betsy," Carly said, refusing to satisfy his curiosity. "Do you want me to carry anything else?"

"Nope. I'll close the cabin and be right behind you."

She went out without looking back. The interior of that cabin was graven indelibly on her mind as it was, and just then, she was doing her best to forget it.

Wally found her staring stonily ahead when he followed her up into the helicopter a few minutes later. He stored the extra rucksack behind him and asked, "All set to go?"

She managed to smile. "As ready as I'll ever be. Are Betsy's innards working properly again?"

"We'll soon find out." He leaned across to fasten the safety latch on her door and then said, "Put on your headphones and fasten your seat belt. Wing was making a fresh pot of coffee when I left."

Carly was able to view the takeoff procedure impassively. She was so anxious to put the night's experience behind her that she would have gladly crawled on a flying carpet just then. She did note that Betsy's roar sounded refreshingly normal before she donned the headphones. "Can we see any of the mountain trail from the air?" she asked after pushing the button on the cord of her headset.

Wally shook his head. "It's in the trees on this side. Why?"

"I was just thinking what a long trip Patrick had on the trail. After you told him that I was stranded." She tacked the last on with some grimness.

The pilot frowned and shot her another puzzled

glance. "What was wrong with that? You *were* stranded—there was no way I could get to you last night. Besides, it wasn't any hardship on Pat."

By then they were halfway around the peak, and Carly gave up trying to see anything of interest on the rocky sides. "I can't think he'd make that trek over the mountain unless he had to."

"What does the trail have to do with it?" Wally pointed toward the end of the lake which encircled the peak. A sliver of silver was visible at the water's edge. "That's what Pat used for transportation."

Carly craned to see before it disappeared beneath them. "I don't understand. What was it?"

"A canoe. Pat had me fly it in at the beginning of the season so we could fish the lake. It's also transportation so the crew can use the cabin in their off-time. Only high-priority passengers like you rate Betsy's services." Wally turned to see Carly's stupefied expression. "My God, you didn't imagine that Pat had to walk all the way? He didn't tell you that, did he?"

Carly rubbed her forehead. "No. He just didn't mention the canoe. I took the other for granted."

"Well, you needn't worry about causing any hardship. If I know Pat, he probably managed some fishing along the way."

Carly remembered the two trout which had appeared providentially for their dinner and felt a surge of anger. Damn the man! Letting her make a bigger fool of herself than she'd imagined. Pretending they were stranded for the night when all the time they could have gone back to the fly camp. No wonder he'd been angry at her refusal to share that miserable cot with him. His carefully laid plans had gone astray, after all.

Her thumb was steady and her voice grimly determined as she pushed the button on her headset cord. "Wally, I want to go back to Ophir today. I'm sure I

can get transportation from there into Fairbanks."
When he opened his mouth to protest, she went on
inexorably, "I think you owe me that. Telling me that
Patrick had okayed my visit to the cabin was a miserable trick, even though you probably meant it for the
best."

"Oh, hell—it was just a gag. Anybody could see that
Pat wanted to get to know you better but he was too
stubborn to admit it. I thought if you just appeared
on the scene, you'd both get a good laugh out of it.
Instead, you're both frothing." Wally leaned forward to tap a dial on the instrument panel. "What
happened last night?"

"I should think you'd have more to do than act like
a keyhole reporter," she observed coolly.

His face took on a ruddy color, showing that her
remark had hit home. "I suppose I deserved that. The
truth is, I hoped to show Laila that Pat had other in-
terests so she might as well look around."

"Your way, for example?"

"Well, yes. Laila has a long list, and right now I'm
at the bottom of it."

The helicopter was approaching the scattered huts
of base camp by then, and Carly could see smoke
coming from the wood stove in the mess hall.
"There's safety in numbers," she told Wally, not really concerned with Laila's love life. "In Fairbanks, she
was hanging on the arm of Craig Norbert. Maybe she
was the reason he changed his plans."

Wally was intent on bringing Betsy to a gentle
touchdown at the landing pad and merely raised his
eyebrows inquisitively.

"I mean it," she insisted. "When I saw him at the
airport the next day, he was scheduled for a flight that
morning, and he mentioned that he was going to be
gone for some time."

The helicopter settled on one skid harder than usual

as the ground came up to meet them, but Wally corrected the left tilt and completed the touchdown with his usual skill. He cut the switches and pulled off his earphones before saying, "So?"

Carly's attention had been diverted, and she looked puzzled until she remembered what she'd been talking about. "Well, when I saw him at Ophir with you, I wondered why he'd changed his plans." Then she went on with a more desperate note. "What about it, Wally? Can you possibly take me in to Ophir today? I don't want to get you in trouble with Patrick, but—" She fell silent as he put up a hand.

"Just a minute. If you saw Craig at the airfield that morning, why didn't you mention it before?"

"Neither of you looked as if you wanted company, so I stayed out of the way." She started to unsnap her seat belt. "It wasn't important. I just wondered why he was still around."

"It was a business deal." Wally appeared deep in thought. "You're serious about wanting to go back to town?"

"Oh, yes!" It might be cowardly of her to choose that action, but just then Carly was too bruised to encounter Patrick again. She half-turned in the seat and said beseechingly to Wally, "You mean you'll take me in to Ophir now?"

"I guess I can." His words were slow and thoughtful. Then, as if he'd made up his mind, he added, "I'll even do better than that. How would you like a nonstop trip to Fairbanks?"

"That would be wonderful!" She stared at him, a faint frown creasing her forehead. "But I don't want to get you in trouble. Patrick wouldn't approve of your taking me that far, would he?"

Wally released his seat belt and opened the helicopter door. "There are some supplies that Pat wanted me to pick up when I had the time. He can't object if

I decide this *is* the time. We'd better be on our way, though. Shall I just go and get your bag?"

"Whatever you say—but won't Wing think it's strange if I don't even say hello?"

"I'll mention that you're not feeling well and anxious to be on the way." Wally jumped to the ground as he spoke.

Carly leaned toward the open door. "Be sure and thank him for me. Tell him that I'm sorry not to say good-bye. He was awfully kind."

"Sure . . . sure." Wally was impatient to get going. "I won't be long. Just wait here."

Carly was left staring after him as he hurried toward the line of tent houses. Once he made up his mind, Wally believed in acting in a hurry. She threaded her fingers through her hair and smoothed it away from her face, wishing she hadn't been counting on Wing's breakfast to make her feel better. At least now she wouldn't have to worry about transportation from Ophir. When she arrived in Fairbanks, there would be time for amenities like food and hot baths. It would give her a chance to arrange an earlier flight south, too. She should be thanking her lucky stars for such a break instead of wishing that she could stay at the base camp. When she remembered how thrilled she'd been to see it the first time, and thought of her undignified retreat now, she could only shake her head.

Wally was back in no time at all, carrying her overnight case in one hand as he loped down the track toward the landing pad. "Wing sends his best," he announced when he pulled open the helicopter door and shoved her bag back with the other gear from the hut. "He would have come down himself except he was baking cinnamon rolls." Wally fumbled in the pocket of his coveralls and pulled out a plastic-wrapped package. "He sent along a sample. Said you needed something to calm your nerves when you were flying with me."

"How nice! I'm starving," Carly said as she unwrapped a still-warm bun. She looked across at Wally, who was strapping himself in. "Did you have one, too?"

"I'll get my share later," he said, intent on his instrument check. "Right now there are other things to do."

Carly thought he was acting far more subdued than usual, but decided to be thankful that she was getting back to Fairbanks without delay. She didn't say anything more and took care to put her earphones on before the takeoff. When they were safely aloft again and Wally seemed intent on his course, she happily devoured the cinnamon bun.

"Feel better?" Wally's question cut through the silence finally.

She carefully wiped the sticky glaze from her fingers before touching the button on her headset cord. "Yes, thanks. Once I corral a cup of coffee, I should make it through the day."

"Sorry. I should have brought a thermos along. Wing probably thought you'd get coffee in Ophir."

"Didn't you tell him we were going straight to Fairbanks?"

Wally's jaw took a more stubborn set. "Pat's the only one who rates explanations."

"You didn't radio him?" she asked, aghast.

"I'll do that later. Why the panic? From the way you talked, he wouldn't give a damn if you were walking barefoot to the North Pole."

"He probably wouldn't." Her chin took a defiant tilt. "I just don't want to complicate things."

"For you or for him? Don't bristle that way," Wally said defensively. "Wing thought I was on the

regular run to Ophir for supplies. We'll be well on
our way to Fairbanks before anyone's the wiser."

Wally piloted the helicopter toward the broad
plateau of the Tanana Valley, keeping Betsy at a
steady cruising level. Carly observed the mammoth
blanket of stunted black spruce trees that she'd noticed on the drive south to Ophir. The only variation
in color beneath them came when a grove of aspen or
birch grew along a winding stream or a small patch of
water. A small plane passed fairly close at one time,
evidently on an IFR—I Follow Roads—flight plan. Not
the best place to be forced down, Carly thought as
she watched the miles pass and gave an involuntary
shudder.

Wally's voice broke into her reverie a little later.
"Shouldn't be long now. You can see the beginnings
of civilization—where that smoke is to the west."

Carly tried to hide her soft sigh of relief. "Do you
have to go and report to the office first thing?"

"I think not." Wally kept his attention fixed
straight ahead. "It's a choice of two evils. Sort of like
that old joke about the guy who has to choose between celibacy or a lobotomy." He went on before
Carly could comment. "I guess I'll be in a better position if I pick up the supplies first and report in afterward. That way, if Pat's unhappy, I'll be able to
refuel and get right back to base camp."

Carly felt a twinge of disappointment, but she
wasn't in a position to argue. "Whatever you say. I
can even help you load them and save time. Where
are they stored?"

"Out by the gold dredge in an all-weather cache a
little north of town."

"I never *did* get back there to do any sketching,"
Carly said, sounding more forlorn than she knew. It
suddenly occurred to her that there were a lot of

things she'd planned before she left Alaska, and now they'd all have to be forgotten.

"Cheer up. Even if you missed your gold dredge, you can see another real Arctic specialty. No extra charge," Wally went on glibly.

"Are you serious?"

He managed to turn and wink at her. "Sure thing. Can't have a visitor missing one of the high points of this country. How many people that you know have ever been in an honest-to-god permafrost tunnel?"

She chewed her lower lip to keep from laughing. "I don't know," she said finally. "The subject of permafrost tunnels doesn't often come up in dinner-table conversation back east."

"Okay, you can be the first on your block to tell about it. As a matter of fact, not many Alaskans have ever been in one. Generally, the tunnels are off-limits except to authorized personnel."

"And your company uses it for a storage depot?" She sounded puzzled.

"Have to. It's the only place with the proper temperature year-round for the storage of explosives. Pat made special arrangements for the use of this place with the Army Engineers."

Despite his glib explanation, Carly still looked puzzled. "I didn't know the army allowed private companies to use their installations."

"Probably they wouldn't, if the place was in active use. This one is partially abandoned. Every once in a while some of the brass come from the Pentagon to make sure their hole in the ground is still here—then they leave us in peace." As he spoke, he was guiding Betsy into a vertical touchdown on a rocky patch near mine tailings that resembled bleak fortifications from above. All that was needed to complete the grim picture was a medieval castle with a gibbet in the courtyard.

The fantasy made Carly frown and say, "I thought this permafrost tunnel was close to town."

As they touched ground, Wally relaxed and started cutting switches. "Fairbanks is only ten miles down the road. The city fathers didn't want explosives stored any closer."

Carly pulled off her headphones and unfastened her seat belt, following his lead. "I can see their point. Are you going to carry explosives with you now?"

"Don't worry." Wally opened his door and grinned crookedly over his shoulder as he started to get out. "You won't have to carry more than a box or two in your lap."

She waited for him to come around and pull open the door on her side before jumping to the ground. "Very funny. What do you do for excitement on the weekend?"

Wally slammed the helicopter door and guided her toward a Quonset hut set close to a small hill a hundred feet away. "I used to go for a drive on Sunday afternoons, but traffic on the freeway scared hell out of me."

"So you took up skydiving instead," she finished for him. "I should have known better than to ask. What's in the Quonset hut?"

"Empty offices." He jerked a thumb toward a rack at the end of it. "We'll borrow a couple of hard hats from the army's supply. It's regulation in the tunnel. The brass don't want to be sued if a rock falls on us."

Carly pulled up beside him at the wooden rack, watching as he selected a white helmet and tried it for size. "This gets better and better," she said faintly. "Are you sure that I need to go inside?"

"Absolutely. A trip in a permafrost tunnel is vital for your education. Orange or white?"

"I beg your pardon?"

"Do you want a white hard hat or an orange one?"

"A thick one." She selected one from the nearest hook, blew the dust from it, and stuck it on her head.

Wally shook his head in mock admiration. "You even look good in that. No wonder you've got Pat . . ." He broke off at her unhappy expression. "Sorry. I didn't mean . . . Oh, hell! Let's get going." He pulled her elbow and led her toward a sturdy gate which was installed in the middle of the hillside.

"I think the place is locked," Carly announced, unable to keep relief from her voice.

"That's okay. I know where there's a key for the padlock. It's stored in this lean-to." Wally left her to detour by a shed at the end of the Quonset hut and came out carrying a key plus two Coleman lanterns. He stopped to survey her waiting figure. "I'll go back to Betsy and get the down vest you had on at the hut. That jacket of yours doesn't look very warm."

"I won't be in the tunnel long enough to matter," she began, but gave up when she saw he was loping back across the gravel to the helicopter, ignoring her protest. He was back again in no time at all, helping her to put the warm vest on over her poplin jacket. Since there was a brisk breeze blowing across the valley, Carly was glad to have the extra covering.

"Thanks, Wally. I'm sorry to put you to so much trouble. Is it much colder in the tunnel?"

"When we get in a ways, the temperature drops to about twenty-two degrees," he said, giving her one lantern and carrying the other as he walked across to unlock the gate.

She shivered and looked around at the deserted installation. "It seems strange that there isn't someone around to check on us. What if we got stuck in there?" She laughed then, despite her fears. "At least we'd be well preserved for posterity."

"Yeah." Wally didn't appear to appreciate the joke. He unlocked the barrier, letting the padlock hang

open on the hasp as he pulled the gate toward her.
"You don't have to worry about this place collaps-
ing—parts of the tunnel go through gravels that have
been here for thirty thousand years."

"And besides, Betsy's big enough and bright enough
to attract some attention in case she's abandoned."
Carly cast a glance over her shoulder at the orange
helicopter before leaving the sunshine and following
Wally into the shadowed tunnel.

He didn't bother to answer her. Instead, he knelt
and lit the two lanterns in the half-daylight provided
by the open gate. As soon as they were burning
brightly, he turned and pulled the barrier closed.

Carly drew in her breath as the gate cut out the last
vestige of daylight. She raised the lantern Wally had
handed her and stared at the shadowed tunnel. It was
big, at least twelve feet high and twenty feet wide.
The walls appeared to be of graveled earth, and the
ground below her feet was powdered sluff which
must have been packed down by traffic and
machinery over the years.

"When the army does something, it's a full-sized
maneuver," Wally said, noting her awed expression as
he stood at her side. "Welcome to the Permafrost
Club."

"I feel as if I should be a mole to qualify." Carly
rubbed the end of her nose vigorously. "From the
smell of things, maybe some moles are still here. Or
are we on the windward side of a fertilizer factory?"

"Stop being so fussy. That's ancient history you're
smelling." Wally caught her elbow and urged her forward. "Come on, let's go deeper. You'll be interested
in the ice crystals down at the end of the tunnel."

"You've convinced me." Carly let herself be led.
"What were the Army Engineers looking for in
here?"

"Nothing special. They did the excavation to test

tunneling equipment in frozen silt and gravel. Permafrost is a unique condition."

"What exactly *is* permafrost?"

"Ground that's permanently below zero degrees Centigrade. You'll see some spectacular ice formations in the silt down here." He gestured toward the side of the tunnel. "There are all sorts of animal bones and decaying organic matter in the muck."

"No gold?" Carly asked. She shivered when the air around them got progressively colder at the deeper level.

"Not that I've heard about. Gold would be found in the gravel layer." He pointed to a mine car in the middle of the tunnel ahead of them. "That was used to haul excavated material out. Just beyond is an old loading machine." He walked over to the wall and held up his lantern. "See those holes? That's the kind they used for drilling and blasting in the gravel."

"Fascinating. No, I mean it. It really *is* interesting," Carly insisted when he gave her a strange look. "But right now I'm hungry, and my feet will be permafrost in about five minutes. Could we just pick up your explosives and be on our way? I promise to walk, not run, to the nearest exit."

"In a minute," he assured her. "There are a couple more things you should see."

The light from their lanterns barely penetrated the shadows in the big cavern which apparently was the end of the tunnel, so it was a relief when Wally walked over beyond another ore car and pulled a switch mounted on a wooden wall support. Immediately light flooded the chamber. For the first time, Carly could appreciate the ice crystals, which looked like a panoply of hoarfrost on the dun-colored muck. "I've never seen anything like it," she said, forgetting her discomfort in the spectacle.

"I told you it was worth a visit. The ice wedges

grow when the ground contracts. They can even be dated—like the rings of a tree." Wally pulled up his cuff and whistled as he checked his watch. "Time for us to be moving."

"Okay. Where are your supplies?"

"Back in this partitioned part." Wally strode toward the end of the tunnel where scrap lumber sectioned off an area. "Have to keep our stuff under lock and key."

"I'm surprised that the environmentalists aren't advocating a permafrost tunnel for every backyard," Carly said, following him. "I can see the ads now—'Be the first on your block to beat pollution. Organic tunnels dug to order.'" She grimaced thoughtfully. "I think they'd sell better if they *weren't* quite so organic. It smells awful in here."

Wally was unlocking the partition door. "You'll get used to it."

"I'd prefer not to stay around that long." She went over and peered past his shoulder at the little room. "It's dark in there. Shall I take the lantern inside?"

"Yeah, do that, will you?" Wally straightened and motioned her inside the partition. "I'll just go back and get a tarp to carry the stuff."

Carly moved into the center of the little room, holding her lantern high to peer into the corners. "I don't see any supplies in here. There's just an empty wooden box and a burlap bag." She walked over to examine it. "Ugh! It smells, too. Are you sure that the army didn't rent this to some grizzly for hibernating last winter?"

The only response to her lighthearted query was the sound of grating metal behind her. She turned, frowning, and gave a stricken gasp when she saw the partition door tightly closed.

An instant later she was pounding on it with her

free hand. "Wally! Wally! This thing's blown shut. Let me out of here!"

By then she'd put the lantern down on the cold earthen floor at her feet and was using both hands to batter the rough wood. She gave up in exhaustion a minute or two later—with only splinters in her fingers and bruised palms to show for her efforts. "Wally!" she shouted again in the still air, and waited vainly for an answer.

Carly took a deep breath, trying to behave rationally and not succumb to the panicky scream that welled in her throat. Evidently the door had swung shut and jammed after Wally had gone back to the tunnel entrance for something he'd forgotten. There was no need to panic—she'd be free again as soon as he returned.

Then she suddenly remembered the sound she'd heard a few minutes before. It wasn't the noise of a door closing—it was metal grating and thudding against wood. Exactly the sound a padlock would make when it was secured in the hasp.

There was no glossing over reality. Wally hadn't gone casually back to the entrance with plans to return. He'd very carefully locked her in before disappearing—and God knows when or if he was ever coming back.

8

That thought was enough to make Carly sink onto the dusty burlap bag wadded on the icy floor. She knew she couldn't stay there long, because the cold started to seep into her flesh almost immediately. Her hands went instinctively under the down vest, giving her a moment of hope as she remembered Wally's insistence that she wear it. Why would he have cared if he hadn't been planning to come back and rescue her soon?

But why did he leave her at all? There'd been nothing in their conversation to make him do such a thing. He'd been amiability itself when telling about the tunnel. Surely he couldn't have been planning to imprison her all along!

Then she remembered how determined he was that she accompany him into the tunnel. And since there weren't any supplies around—at least that she could see—the whole maneuver must have been fabricated. But why?

Carly rubbed her forehead with cold fingers and tried to remember what had happened since Wally rescued her at the lake. Surely her unhappiness with Patrick didn't have anything to do with it. She let out a soft moan of unhappiness when she even thought of Patrick. If only she hadn't been so intent on getting away! As far as he knew, she was safely at base camp. There wasn't much hope that he'd even care enough to check on her whereabouts. It would be evening, at least, before Wing would report that she wasn't in camp.

That thought was depressing enough to make Carly scramble to her feet. So the prospect looked grim—at least she didn't have to collapse like a wet paper bag.

All sorts of things could happen, she told herself as she started some vigorous calisthenics to get her circulation going. Wally could be back in minutes. Maybe he just had another meeting planned nearby that he didn't want observed—like that earlier one at Ophir with Craig Norbert.

Carly stopped so abruptly in the middle of her exercise that she looked like a stick figure with her arms at a ludicrous angle. She lowered them slowly, shoving her hands in her pockets while she thought about that clandestine get-together on the airfield. Of course! That was the only thing that had really upset Wally on the flight. In fact, it was right after she'd mentioned it that he'd suggested bringing her into town.

That could mean Craig was close at hand. Carly's thoughts took another dip as she realized she must have been the only witness to that other meeting. It was entirely possible that Craig wouldn't be any happier about it than Wally.

The conclusion was enough to make her slump despairingly against the door—but only for an instant. Things were bad enough without trying to add to her predicament, she told herself angrily. All she had to do was keep as warm as possible while figuring out a way to escape.

She scowled as she looked around; she was no match for the sturdy walls. Even if she beat on them with a piece of scrap lumber for hours, they wouldn't budge. The time factor made her bend and check the fuel in the lantern. Thank heaven, light wouldn't be a problem for a while. She could be grateful to Wally for not taking the lantern with him. If she were locked in without light, she'd be in hysterics by now.

Well, she wasn't going into hysterics, she told herself. Not by a long shot. Not while there was anything she could do.

She stamped her feet to try to warm them, wrinkling her nose as she saw silt rise in the lantern's gleam. Then her glance narrowed abruptly. Silt was dirt. Even if it was frozen dirt, she could at least make a dent in it. The partition walls wouldn't have any foundation. She'd bet on it!

By then she was scrabbling through the scrap lumber in the corner. If she gouged and scraped at the frozen silt with a piece of it, she could dig a hole under the partition.

It didn't need *The Guinness Book of Records* to tell her that her chances were slim; her half-frozen feet and hands told her that already. But it certainly made more sense than wasting her strength doing exercises. Carly's chin firmed in a way that Patrick would have recognized as she bent to her task.

She lost track of time as she scraped and piled the icy dirt she was able to dislodge. When her fingers became too cold and painful, she wrapped them in burlap and knelt to start again.

It was exhaustion which finally forced her to sink against the wall. Surely she must have dug halfway under it, she rationalized, as she allowed her eyelids to come down for just a moment. Now she had to scrape out enough dirt to reach the surface on the other side of the partition.

Her head rolled restlessly against the rough wall. Dear God, it was so cold, so hard to dig where you couldn't see.

Tears slid down her cheeks, but she made no attempt to wipe them away. That would acknowledge her weakness. Besides, it was better to keep her chilled hands under the down vest in an attempt to warm them.

That was the last coherent thought she had.

Much later, when there were masculine voices in the tunnel and finally the sound of the door's hinges being removed, it didn't really penetrate her fogged mind.

She was barely conscious of being scooped up in some stranger's arms and carried for a distance. Her first semblance of normalcy came when they emerged in the sunlight. She managed to open her eyes as she was lowered onto a bench outside the Quonset hut by the tunnel entrance.

"I didn't think anything could feel so good," she murmured, trying to sit up and identify the two uniformed men staring down at her.

"What's that, Miss Marshall?" asked the officer who'd carried her.

Carly surveyed his middle-aged, weather-beaten face and decided she'd never seen anything nicer. "The sunshine," she said in a thick voice. "It's the real gold, isn't it?"

If he felt she was still a little incoherent, he was considerate enough to hide it. "That's right," he said in a kindly tone, "but sometimes people get their priorities mixed." He knelt to take off her shoes and started briskly rubbing her icy feet and ankles. "Are you okay until we can have a doctor run his rule over you?"

"I don't need a doctor. I'm all right—or will be in a minute." As her circulation improved under his ministrations, she grimaced with pain. "Ouch! It feels like there are a million needles jabbing me. I think it was better before."

"That's where you're wrong." He shot her a keen glance. "Are both feet the same?"

She nodded, realizing then what he meant. "Yes . . . thanks. I shouldn't have fallen asleep. But I got so tired . . ." Her voice trailed off as she suddenly looked around. "Did Wally call you? Is he here?"

The other uniformed officer who was watching gave a snort of laughter. "Burton won't be out calling for quite a while." When Carly stared in bewilderment, he went on in a more kindly tone. "He and Craig Norbert are in custody. There's not much chance of their getting back on the street for some time."

Carly started to brush back her hair but stopped when she saw how filthy her fingers were. She sat up straighter and rubbed her hand against her jeans instead. "I feel as if I'd missed the first installment. What did Craig and Wally do?" Her eyes grew wide as a thought occurred to her. "They didn't take those gold nuggets, did they?"

Both officers grinned at that. The one in front of Carly started to put her shoes back on. "Not likely. Norbert and Burton had a more lucrative racket going." He got to his feet then and helped her up. "Let's get you back to town."

"Just a minute." She resisted his gentle nudge toward the police car parked at the other end of the hut. "What was Wally involved in? It must have been something awful for him to leave me in that tunnel."

"Transporting drugs fits into that category," the

older officer told her, urging her toward the car again. "It's about as low as a man can get."

Carly stared at his grim face. "Are you sure he's guilty?" she asked in a thin voice. Then before he could reply, she said, "I can't believe it. Why would Wally do such a thing?"

"For money, Miss Marshall. The payoff must have been terrific," the younger officer said, opening the car door. "Better wrap up in that blanket on the back seat until you get good and warm."

Carly climbed in, automatically following his instructions.

He shut the door behind her and got into the front beside the other officer. "We'll need a statement from you, but I imagine you'd like to get cleaned up first. We can drop you by the hospital for an emergency-room checkup—"

"No . . . please," Carly interrupted. "Honestly, I'm all right. As soon as I have a hot bath, I'll be as good as new."

"Well, if you're sure." The older officer gave her an appraising glance as he pulled the car out onto the arterial and headed toward Fairbanks. "We'll take you home then and you can give us a statement later."

"Fine. I'm staying at my sister's place. It's—"

"—Pat Donovan's house," the officer cut in. "He told us."

"But how could he? He isn't here. He can't be," she finished wildly.

"He doesn't have to be." The younger officer gave her a comradely grin over his shoulder. "Donovan contacted us by radio. That's how we knew you were missing in the first place."

"I thought Wally sent you to rescue me."

"Then you thought wrong." The officer behind the wheel was calm and decisive. "Burton didn't volunteer a thing until he figured some cooperation might get him a lighter sentence. Pat had already told us that you were aboard the helicopter. Naturally we were curious when Burton landed at the airport alone."

"I'm surprised he went there at all," Carly said. "Why didn't he pick a more secluded place?"

"It's a little hard to hide an orange helicopter in the tundra. Besides, Burton had no idea we were waiting for him. He was scheduled to meet Norbert for the payoff on their last drug shipment. Probably he suspected it might be the final one. Norbert admitted that when we arrested him earlier this morning. He said Burton had gotten beaten up the other night by some of their business competitors as a warning."

"They must have been gunning for Wally when that shot came in the kitchen. He'd brought me back to the house earlier."

The younger officer nodded. "I read the report on that. It all fits. They probably caught up with Burton later and worked him over."

"But how did you learn about Craig Norbert's part in it?"

"An informant. That's the most common way. Norbert could transport the contraband on his regular flight schedule. And did—until he overreached his luck. When he was arrested early this morning, he couldn't wait to start passing the blame around. All we had to do was wait for Burton to drop in. Literally."

Carly smiled crookedly in response. It was either laugh or cry at that moment, and she'd done far too much of the latter. "I'm astonished that Mr. Donovan found out about it so fast."

Her reply surprised the younger officer. "Pat didn't radio because of the drug bust—he just wanted to reach Burton so he could get hold of you. When he learned what was happening here, he didn't waste any time. He informed us that he wanted you found pronto." The man's rugged face creased in laughter. "He also ordered us to hang onto you, but the chief told him he'd need to swear out a warrant for that. If you've run off with the camp silver, Miss Marshall, you'd better give it back. Pat was mighty upset."

Carly didn't try to find an answer for that. It appeared she was more firmly entrenched in Patrick's doghouse than ever. Probably because she'd hitch-hiked a ride on an unauthorized flight in his precious helicopter. Wally had mentioned what Betsy's time cost, and it had made her shudder. Now it seemed she wasn't the only one to have a violent reaction.

"You feeling okay?"

Her head came up in surprise at the question from the front seat. "Yes, much better—thanks."

"You didn't look it. Sure you don't want to drive by the hospital? There's still time to detour that way."

"No, really." She chose her next words carefully. "Actually, I'd hoped to leave town this afternoon. If I can get reservations on a flight to Anchorage, will it be all right with you?"

The older officer met her glance in the rear-vision mirror. "We'll need a statement first. The police here don't approve of people being abandoned in freezing tunnels. You were lucky this time. If you'd been there longer, you'd be missing some vital parts. Like feet and hands."

His brutal summing-up made Carly swallow nervously. "I know. I promise you that I'll sign the statement, but I'd still like to leave today if it's possible."

"I can't blame you for that. Probably be the best thing for you. Go somewhere and enjoy the rest of your vacation." He saw her raised eyebrows and grinned again. "Oh, yes—Pat told us about that, too. There's nothing sacred in a small town. Makes our job a little easier."

If that was true, Carly thought she might as well take advantage of it. "Did Mr. Donovan mention when he was coming back to town?"

The two men stared blankly at each other, and then the one on the right shrugged and shook his head. "I don't think so. Why? Is it important?"

"No. Not really. You said that he wanted you to hang onto me. I wondered why." She smiled then, wryly. "Since I didn't steal the silver."

"Probably he thought you'd need rest after the early flight. We'll tell him that you're okay if he checks with headquarters again."

Carly found she'd have to be satisfied with that as the two men started talking about a law-enforcement seminar they were planning to attend in Anchorage. She stared through the dusty window of the patrol car, trying to keep her mind a careful blank. Once she got clean and had something hot to drink, she'd be able to cope again. Until then, it wouldn't take much to make her start howling.

It was ironic to be feeling like a basket case when she should be setting off rockets over the fact that she was still alive. She hadn't needed that discreet rebuke from her rescuers to know how fortunate she was to emerge unscathed from the icy tunnel. Now, instead of being grateful, she was moping because she couldn't have it all ways. And even if Patrick were in town, she told herself firmly, he wouldn't welcome her sobbing on his shoulder.

"Here we are." It was the younger policeman this time who spoke up. "Looks as if everything's in good shape at your house. At least you won't have to worry about target practice on the kitchen window again."

"That's something." Carly was trying to disentangle her feet from the blanket when he opened the rear door of the car. She scanned the familiar outlines of the house, surprised to find how glad she was to see it—even if for only a little while.

She took a deep breath of the clear spring air as she was helped out of the car, resolving never to complain about the weather again. The sunshine felt marvelous and the cloudless sky was a blue that deserved every adjective in the book.

The two officers deliberately lingered on the curb beside her—as if they realized her need to savor the surroundings for a moment longer.

When she smiled apologetically at them, the older officer gestured toward the kitchen door. "Got your key?" he asked, bringing things blessedly back to normal.

She patted her jacket pocket. "That's about all I *do* have. I left everything else in the helicopter."

"We'll have somebody drop your stuff by. Give us a call when it's convenient."

Carly nodded agreement. "Or I can pick it up when I come down and sign that statement." She hesitated on the back steps after unlocking the door. "Did I ever thank you for saving my life?"

For the first time since she'd met them, the officers appeared ill-at-ease.

"We'll take it as read," the older man said. "If there's anything else we can do, just call."

He gave her a casual salute, and as they turned back toward the car, the younger one winked over his shoulder. "Standard procedure for beautiful taxpayers. See you."

The men's reluctance to take her seriously made Carly smile as she went in the kitchen and closed the door behind her. Their response had been just what she needed. Her absent glance lit on the refrigerator at that moment, and her smile widened. Food was what she really needed to stiffen her backbone—even more than bracing comments.

The first swallow of milk was sheer ambrosia, and she carried a glass with her even as she put on the kettle to heat water for coffee. She thought of frying bacon and decided against it, settling for buttered toast dripping with honey. The water boiled in time to provide a wonderful finale. As she sniffed the fragrance of brewed coffee she decided that French perfumers had definitely overlooked a winner.

It was surprising how much better she felt afterward. The morning's events were still enough to make her shudder, but at least she could now face the rest of the day without dissolving into tears. By the time she had a shower and found some clean clothes, she should feel even better.

She packed away her jeans and shirt, thinking if she never saw them again it would be too soon. From now on, it was back to civilized clothes. If she got to Hawaii or Fiji, there was no reason she couldn't buy a couple of outfits for the beach.

Her decision didn't work the miracle she hoped for. The truth was, she really didn't want to go to Hawaii or Fiji or anywhere just then. But she also knew that she couldn't stand meeting Patrick again. And once Nancy returned, he was bound to reappear. It would be less embarrassing for both of them if she fabricated a plausible excuse and disappeared.

Carly turned on the shower and tried to decide what kind of a note she would leave for Nancy. Probably it would be easiest to say she was called back to New York because of her work.

By the time she'd stepped under the shower, she was almost convinced that returning east was the easiest solution. It was silly to waste time and money taking a vacation when she would probably sit on a beach by herself and wallow in self-pity.

She was out of the shower by that time, wrapped in one towel and drying her hair with another. Since the cabinet mirror was fogged with steam, she used still another towel to clear the surface and then made a face at her reflection. Her hair was still damp but she ran a comb through it and decided it would have to do. At least that horrible tunnel dust was gone. Even a fleeting thought of it made her shudder, and she reached in the cabinet for Nancy's sandalwood body lotion, smoothing it over her arms and shoulders. The delicate fragrance rose from her warm skin and Carly gave a satisfied nod as she replaced the bottle.

It took just a minute for her to hang up the damp towels and pull on the sprigged challis robe she had hanging on a hook. She was halfway into the bedroom to get her scuffs when she heard a knock on the kitchen door.

"Damn!" she murmured, wishing people could get in and out of a shower without the telephone ringing or the doorbell buzzing. She slipped into the scuffs and went over to the bedroom door, calling, "Just a minute—I'll be right there."

She didn't wait for a response. If whoever it was didn't hear her and went away, it wouldn't be a tragedy.

Her quick glance at the bedroom mirror revealed the flimsy challis wrap wasn't suitable for greeting door-to-door salesmen. Then she remembered a terry kimono hanging in the closet.

She was pulling it off the hanger when she heard decisive footsteps in the hallway. The bedroom door was suddenly shoved open with such force that it slammed against the wall.

Patrick stood frowning on the threshold.

9

It was hard to tell which of them was more un-
nerved by the confrontation. Carly's breathless "Oh,
Lord!" disappeared under Patrick's astounded "Why
in the devil didn't you say you were here!"

Carly recovered first. "If you didn't think I was
here, why did you knock?"

"I knocked because I thought you might be, but
when there was no answer, I—"

"—came in to call."

"Something like that," he admitted, the color rising
under his cheekbones.

Carly was trying to keep both her temper and the
edges of her challis robe under control. "That doesn't
even make sense."

Patrick looked drawn—as if he'd spent the last
twenty-four hours without sleep—but it hadn't fazed
his temper. "You should talk about making sense!
Anybody who was fool enough to climb into a helicopter without even leaving a message. My God, if

Wing hadn't kept his eyes open, we wouldn't have known where to start looking."

He moved toward her like a sleepwalker, pulling the terry kimono from her nerveless clasp and tossing it on the bed. "Why are you running around half-dressed now? The police said you were almost frozen in that tunnel when they found you. I should think you'd try to stay warm." He reached out with a probing finger. "Dammit all, your hair's even wet."

"Dammit all yourself!" she flared back. "If you'd get out of here, I could dry it." The lump came back to her throat then and she was horrified to feel tears welling up. She turned her back on him deliberately as she searched for a handkerchief in the pocket of her robe. It was an effort to keep her voice level, but she managed. "I'm sorry I inconvenienced you this morning. As soon as I can arrange a plane reservation this afternoon, I'll be out of your way permanently."

There was an ominous silence. Then Patrick's voice came, distinct and dry. "You won't get out of this house—let alone out of town."

Carly couldn't believe what she'd heard, and she turned back to face him, her lovely eyes glistening with tears.

Patrick was no proof against such delicate beauty. "I should beat you within an inch of your life," he muttered roughly, and folded her in his arms. "But right now, I don't have the energy."

His clasp was a combination of torture and bliss for Carly. She would have given anything to relax in the warm security of that embrace, but she remembered all too well what his touch had done to her defenses in the cabin. Those strong hands had moved with sensuous sureness then, and left her weak with desire. She tried to turn away, knowing that it would happen again, and this time she lacked the strength or inclination to resist.

Patrick's grip tightened at once. He must have been aware of her conflict, because his clasp stayed gentle; he seemed content just to hold her, to make her relax and mold her soft body against his.

When he felt her resistance give way, as if she was too tired to oppose him any longer, he spoke softly. "I thought I'd lose my mind after they said that Wally had landed without you. It took forever to borrow a plane at Ophir and get here. I didn't find out you were all right until we landed a half-hour ago." He rested his cheek against her hair. "It was agony all the way."

Carly felt warmth run through her. She slipped her arms around his waist then and pressed even closer. "I didn't think I'd ever see you again," she whispered. "That was the worst part for me."

"And whose fault was that?" He cupped her face and forced her to look up at him. "Idiot!" He kissed her softly. "Darling idiot." That time the kiss wasn't soft at all.

Carly burrowed her nose in his shirtfront again when he finally lifted his head. She had to cling because her knees felt like *blanc mange* and otherwise she would have collapsed at his feet. "I hope this is real," she murmured. "Everything else about today has been a nightmare. I'm almost afraid to open my eyes."

Patrick's hands moved, making her vibrantly aware of their strength through the thin fabric of her robe. "It's no dream," he assured her in a deep voice. "I can think of a couple surefire ways to prove it."

"I'll take your word for it," Carly responded breathlessly, putting her hands over his to halt his progress, although she knew that he could feel her heartbeat rocket under his touch.

"You do that." He kept his hands quiet, but they stayed where they were.

"Did the police tell you what happened?" Carly did her best to ask something that would make sense. It was difficult because all she wanted just then was to pull his head down so that he could kiss her again. "I still can't see why somebody like Craig Norbert would be involved in something as ghastly as running drugs. He had a good job . . . he seemed nice. Awfully nice."

"Who knows?" Pat's voice was quiet, as if he knew there was no need to hurry things. "He had the opportunity. Laila said that he was flying a run to the Far East last year. Probably the chance of so much money swayed his judgment."

"Was she upset when she heard about it?"

He nodded. "She was at the airport when we landed. Looked as if she was in a state of shock."

Carly kept her eyes down. "And you didn't mind?"

Her voice didn't give anything away, but Pat tightened his clasp to administer a gentle shake. "Why should I? Laila works for me, that's all."

"It looked like more than that when you were at base camp."

His shoulders shook with laughter. "Self-defense. Remember, I'd just seen Wally making a pass at you."

"That was a surprise to me, too. I think he tried to show Laila that he was spreading his favors around . . ." She broke off to add, "You were annoyed before that."

"Because you were late arriving. I thought that . . . God knows what I thought," he admitted.

She reached up to smooth the stern line of his chin. "That wasn't my fault. Wally had been chauffeuring Craig around while I cooled my heels at Ophir."

Patrick's eyes kindled at her touch, but his voice was still stern. "Why didn't you mention it then, for Pete's sake?"

This time, it was Carly who chuckled. "You didn't give me a chance. The temperature dropped ten degrees in twenty seconds."

"I was jealous. I'd never felt that way before. It sure as hell plays havoc with a man's peace of mind." He dropped a swift kiss at the deep V neckline of her robe. "Along with other things."

Carly shivered but managed to say, "When I saw the possessive way that Laila was acting with you, I could have gone for her jugular vein. I'd never felt that way before, either. I couldn't understand why I did then."

"Especially since you'd cast me as the villain of the piece."

"Fine villain! Troth I like him wondrously," she quoted. "That was the trouble all along, and I suspected it."

"So did I." His lips were insistent at the hollow of her throat. "When Wally told me that you'd insisted on going to the cabin, I couldn't believe my luck. I should have been suspicious, but—"

"—it was the best offer you'd had all day . . ." She broke off as he nipped her promptly. "Brute!"

He grinned, unrepentant. "Maybe you're right. At any rate, when you thought we were marooned there overnight, I decided to go along with the idea."

"And not rock the canoe?" She watched him wince with every evidence of enjoyment. "Playing charades about catching those fish! What did you do—go get trout out of your icebox at the fly camp?"

"I'd caught them earlier," he admitted. "They were still in the canoe."

"I haven't forgiven you for that dodge." She tightened the belt on her robe and moved prudently to arm's length.

He responded with a slow grin. "I did my best to

make amends later. Why in the deuce do you think I left you alone last night? Once I learned that Wally had gotten you there under false pretenses, I couldn't take advantage of the situation. A man and a woman should both know the rules of the game. After that, they can decide whether they want to take part."

"You needn't spell it out," she said, sounding embarrassed. "But I wish you'd explained then."

"I wasn't in the mood for explanations. I was lucky to even make it through the front door after what happened. As it was I spent the hours until daylight trying to figure out what the devil had happened to me. Ever since I'd met you, I'd been walking around in a fog. At first, I thought leaving Fairbanks would solve everything. Then I got scared something might happen to you if you stayed alone here at the house. The possibility that you might leave town before I came back was even worse." He paused to add, "As long as we're clearing the slate, I'd better tell you that I haven't spent any nights in this house while Nancy's had the lease. I have an apartment down the block."

"You let me think you used that upstairs bedroom all the time," she accused.

"Hell, I never even thought about it until you arrived! Then it seemed like a good idea to stick around. I didn't try to figure out why."

"But then we went from bad to worse." She gave him a tremulous look. "Until now."

He reached for her again to pull her close. "Things are going to be even more difficult now."

"What do you mean?"

"Just that. We have three days to wait until we can get married. By then, Nancy and Hal should be here to stand up with us. But in the meantime, that bed over there looks more inviting by the minute." He jerked his head toward the piece of furniture in question. "It's going to be the very devil staying away from it."

Carly bit her lip to keep from laughing as she pretended to consider it. "Especially since you threatened not to let me out of the house."

"That's right." Patrick's glance glinted with mischief. "I've left Toklat on guard at the kitchen door."

Carly raised her eyebrows and walked over to check. She opened the bedroom door and peered out. A second later, she straightened and closed it firmly behind her.

"I warned you," Patrick said smugly. "Tok's a top-flight guard dog."

Her lips twitched. "We'll have to send him back to obedience school for a refresher course, then. He just woke up long enough to wag his tail."

"Damn! Outmaneuvered again." Patrick sighed and reached around her for the doorknob. "I'll go put on some coffee while you get dressed." He lingered a moment longer before opening the door. "If that's what you want."

When Carly didn't answer right away, he put out his hand and ran one finger lightly down over the front of her robe. His eyes didn't miss her trembling response, but he waited, unmoving, for her decision.

She stared at him for an instant. Then she reached up to frame his face with her palms and survey him lovingly. "There's no hurry about the coffee," she said in a husky voice. "I'd rather have you stay and tell me where we're going to live—important things like that."

He bent to brush his lips against hers. "A very sound idea. But first, my dearest one, I'll tell you how much I love you. That might take a while—what with one thing and another."

"Especially with one thing and another . . ."

It was all she had a chance to say. By then, Patrick

was showing her that action was far better than words. The way he was going about it, it was certainly going to take a while.

How wonderful they had a lifetime to spend!

About the author

Glenna Finley is a native of Washington State. She earned her degree from Stanford University in Russian Studies and in Speech and Dramatic Arts, with emphasis on radio.

After a stint in radio and publicity work in Seattle, she went to New York City to work for NBC as a producer in its international division. In addition, she worked with the "March of Time" and *Life* magazine.

As a producer, she had her own show about activities in Manhattan, a show that was broadcast to England. The programs were similar to those of the "Voice of America."

Though her life in New York was exciting, she eventually returned to the Northwest where she married. Currently residing in Seattle with her husband, Donald Witte, and their son, she loves to travel, and draws heavily on her travels and experiences for the novels that have been published. Her books for NAL have sold several million copies.